Alfred John Church

Stories of the Magicians

Thalaba and the Magicians of the Domdaniel, Rustem and the Genii, Kehama and

his Sorceries

Alfred John Church

Stories of the Magicians
Thalaba and the Magicians of the Domdaniel, Rustem and the Genii, Kehama and his Sorceries

ISBN/EAN: 9783744749732

Printed in Europe, USA, Canada, Australia, Japan

Cover: Foto ©Andreas Hilbeck / pixelio.de

More available books at **www.hansebooks.com**

STORIES

OF

THE MAGICIANS

THALABA *and the* MAGICIANS *of the* DOMDANIEL
RUSTEM *and the* GENII
KEHAMA *and his* Sorceries

BY THE

REV. ALFRED J. CHURCH, M.A.

Professor of Latin in University College, London
Author of " Stories from Homer "

With Sixteen Illustrations

LONDON
SEELEY & CO., 46, 47 & 48, ESSEX STREET, STRAND
(*LATE OF* 54, *FLEET STREET*)
1887

CONTENTS

CONTENTS.

THE STORY OF RUSTEM.

THE STORY OF KEHAMA.

LIST OF ILLUSTRATIONS.

PREFACE.

SOUTHEY'S Oriental Romances, *Thalaba the Destroyer* and *The Curse of Kehama*, are, I suppose, almost wholly unknown to the younger generation of readers. It must be confessed that they are not commended by their metrical form; but they display great power of imagination, and convey an admirable moral. I have tried to tell these two stories in prose.

I have added the *Story of Rustem*, greatly condensed, from Firdausi's *Shah-Nameh*, or *Book of the Kings*. I have availed myself of M. Jules Mohl's translation from the Persian, a popular edition of which, in seven octavo volumes, was published under the care of Madame Mohl in the years 1876–8. It was necessary to take some liberties with the story, for the chief of which I may plead the authority of Mr. Matthew Arnold, who, in his beautiful poem of "Sohrab and Rustem," represents the father as believing that the child born to him by his Tartar wife is a girl. In Firdausi's poem he knows that he has a son, but cannot believe that so young a child can be his stalwart antagonist.

The illustrations are taken from Persian and Indian MSS. in the British Museum.

Hadley Green,
    Sept. 21, 1886.

THE STORY OF THALABA.

CHAPTER I.

THE MEETING OF THE MAGICIANS.

MANY years ago there was in Arabia a great Society of very powerful magicians. These by diligent practice of their art had learnt such spells that they could do almost what they would, even to making the sun dark at noonday. There was no end to the wickedness that they did, and the whole country groaned from the tyranny which they exercised upon it. These magicians had their chief meeting-place in a great cave under the sea, which was called the Domdaniel cavern ; and here, when this story begins, they were assembled to deliberate about a very grave matter. It had been revealed to them by their art that a child had been born in Arabia who should destroy

them and their dwelling, unless indeed they
could first kill him. Further, they had learnt
that this child was the son of a certain
Hodeirah, an Arab chief who lived in the
desert. Knowing this, the heads of the
Society assembled together, and drew lots
who should go to kill Hodeirah and his wife
and children. He had eight children, and as
the magicians did not know who among the
eight should be the Destroyer, it was needful
that all should be slain. One of the Society,
whose name was Okba, drew the lot, and went
immediately to do his errand, and the others
waited till he should return ; and as he could
transport himself by his art in a moment of
time whithersoever he would, they had no need
to wait long.

There were three that sat together in the
cavern ; that is to say, three of greater note
than the rest, namely, Khawla, the witch, and
Lobaba, and Abdaldar. Before these three
burned ten flames, that sprang up from the
rocky floor of the cavern, and burned without
fuel.. One flame was the life of Hodeirah, and
one the life of Zeinab his wife, and there was a

flame for the life of each of his eight children. "Burn flames," cried Abdaldar, "burn while the race of Hobdeirah lives." As they looked the flames began to grow dim and to waver. "Curse on him!" cried Khawla the witch, "curse on Okba's hasty hand! The fool has failed; eight only are gone out."

So saying, she turned to inquire of the Teraph, or oracle, which the magicians had set up in their cave. This oracle was the head of a child, fixed on a plate of gold, and on the plate was written the name of an evil spirit. Only the eyes had life, and the mouth could speak. "Tell me," she said, "is the fire gone out that threatens the race of the magicians?"

The head answered, "The fire yet lives."

At that moment came Okba, bearing in his hand a dagger dripping with blood. "See the flames, Okba," said Khawla the witch. "See how they burn; and you know that while they burn, we are in danger. Did your heart fail you? Could you not see? A curse on your weakness."

"Khawla," said Okba, "you should have known me better. Eight times I struck, and

I struck home; there needed no second blow. But when I would have struck the ninth time, there came a cloud about me, and my eyes could see nothing. I struck through the cloud with my dagger, and the dagger was driven back upon myself, and I heard a voice that said, 'Cease, son of Perdition. Thou canst not change what is written in the book of fate.'"

Then Khawla turned again to the oracle. "Tell me," she said, "where our enemy is hidden."

The dead lips answered, "I behold the sea, and I behold the land, but the boy is neither on the sea nor on the land."

Lobaba said, "A power that is mightier than we are protects him; but see! one of the Fires burns dim! see, it quivers! it goes out!"

As he spoke, the ninth fire went out; and only the tenth was left, a pale blue flame that seemed to tremble on the floor, as if the darkness would have swallowed it up. But while the magicians looked it grew and grew and spread over all the space where the ten had been. And from thence it extended itself over the whole cave, so that the eyes of the Teraph, which before had shone so brightly, were dim in comparison with it; and the faces of the magicians were ghastly pale as they looked at it.

Khawla was the first that regained her courage. She called up the chief of the evil spirits that were her servants, and said, " Tell me, Spirit, where lives the boy whose life is in the fire that burns before us ? "

The Spirit said, " I cannot see him either on the sea or on the earth. Ask some believing spirit; I cannot answer thee."

" Bring Hodeirah," said Khawla; and, in a moment, so mighty were her spells, the dead man was laid at her feet, with the blood not yet clotted on his wound, and in his hand the sword which he had grasped in his death.

"Art thou in Paradise ? " said Khawla, "or art thou under the throne of Allah ? Wherever thou art, thou shalt hear my voice and obey."

And she muttered spells so terrible and so strong that Heaven itself trembled to hear them. And as she muttered them, the eye-balls began to roll and the lips to quiver. She rejoiced to see that her spells had such power, and cried, " Hodeirah, tell me where is thy son ?"

Hodeirah groaned and shut his eyes. "Speak!" cried Khawla again. "Answer me, or thou shalt live for hundreds of years in torture."

Hodeirah cried, "God deliver me from this agony." "Speak!" cried Khawla again, and snatched a viper from the ground and lashed him with it. But in that moment Allah heard his prayer, and Khawla had nothing but a corpse on which to wreak her rage. Then the fire spread from its place, and wrapped the body about with flames, and consumed both flesh and bones. But the sword was left. Then Khawla said, " The boy must be slain ; but before he can be slain, he must be found. Let us draw lots who shall go and seek for him."

So they took the arrows of chance, and held them loosely in their hands with their points towards the flame. In a little time the arrow which Abdaldar held began to point to him. So the task fell to the lot of Abdaldar. He was to search through every tribe that dwelt in Arabia ; not a solitary tent was he to leave unvisited till the boy should be found.

But how should he know the boy? The way that he contrived was this. He had a wonderful ring upon his finger, and in the ring a stone that was more wonderful still. It was made of dew that had been frozen in the very beginning of the world, and had lain with the whole weight of the Caucasus mountains upon it till it had become as blue as the sea. With this ring Abdaldar approached the fire, and caused by his spells that a spark of it should enter into the stone, for he knew that when he should put his hand having this ring on it upon the boy, the spark of fire would go out of the stone. For, being a part of the Boy's life, it would join itself at once to that to which it belonged. So Abdaldar set about his search.

CHAPTER II.

ASWAD.

WHERE then was Thalaba that the Spirit could not see him either on the land or on the sea? When Hodeirah and his children were slain by Okba the Magician, Zeinab fled into the desert with Thalaba, the one son that was left to her, a lad of some twelve years of age. It was night, and she wandered on, not knowing where she was going or what she should do.

"Mother," said Thalaba, "tell me who slew my father?"

"I know not," answered Zeinab, "I did not think that he had an enemy."

"Well, I will hunt him through the world. Already I can bend my father's bow, and I shall soon have strength to drive an arrow into his heart."

"All that is far in the future, my son; but now we are in the desert."

And she looked round, but could not see even a tree; only the dark blue sky closing them round on every side like a great dome. She thought to herself, "Why were we saved? we shall die here of hunger and thirst;" and she sat down and wept over the boy.

A moment after he cried out in wonder, and Zeinab lifted up her head, and saw before her a great palace in the midst of a wood. The trees were such that the very cedars of Lebanon could not match them, and the palace more splendid than any that had ever been built in Egypt or Babylon or Rome. The two went into the wood, and walked on till, under the shade of a mimosa tree, they saw a young man lying on a couch. He had been asleep, but woke at the sound of their steps, and looked with wonder at the new-comers.

"Forgive us," said Zeinab, "distress has made me bold. Help us; God blesses them that help the widow and the fatherless."

"Thank God," said the young man, "that I hear again a human voice. But tell me, who are you that you have found your way into this place which no foot of man has trodden for ages ?"

"Yesterday," said Zeinab, "I was a happy wife and mother. To-day I am a widow, and of my children this only is left."

"Heaven has surely guided you hither," cried the young man, "and lifted the veil which has hidden this place for many ages from the eyes of men. But hear my tale."

"This is the Paradise of Irem which King Shedad built in his pride. In the days of my youth this was a populous land and rich. The tribe of Ad inhabited it, and there was none whose sons were braver or daughters more fair. My name then was Aswad—what ages have passed since I heard it! I was of noble birth and rich. My father had a hundred horses in his stables ; as for the number of his camels it was not known. We were prosperous and powerful, but alas! we worshipped idols, and we mocked the prophets of God when they bade us turn from our evil ways and repent.

"King Shedad conceived in his heart the desire to make a garden in the wilderness more beautiful than the Garden of Eden, and to build in the middle of the Garden a palace which should surpass all the palaces upon earth. For this palace gold mines were exhausted, and precious stones, diamonds, and emeralds and rubies and sapphires were gathered from all the world, and ebony, that strange tree which has neither fruit nor leaves, but grows under the earth, where it is discovered by its scent. In the garden there were all the flowers that are known in the world. The trees Shedad transplanted full grown, for he was not content to wait. And in every walk of the garden there were marble statues of chiefs and heroes. Long since the statues have become mere shapeless lumps of stone, but the trees and the flowers remain, for the care of nature has perpetuated them. When the palace and the garden were finished, there came a great drought upon the country of the children of Ad. For three years there was no rain, till the wells were dried up. We prayed for rain, but we prayed to our idols; and it was all in vain. There was neither rain nor dew. At last the King sent a messenger, Kail by name, to the

Red Hillock at Mecca, thinking that the gods would hear our prayers more readily from there. And all the while the prophet Houd, who was a messenger of the true God, continued to warn us, crying, 'Turn, ye men of Ad, from the wrath to come;' but we gave no heed to him.

"At this time it chanced that my father died, and was buried. At his grave, after the custom of the country, we tied a camel, and left it to die, that when the resurrection came, he might find it ready to mount. It was his favourite beast, and it had carried me often when I was a child, and one day as I passed by, it knew me, and turned its eye upon me. Sunk it was and dim, for the beast was nearly dead of hunger. I could not bear to see it, and taking my knife, I cut the rope, and let it go free, thinking that there was no man near to see what I did. But Houd the prophet saw me, and said, 'Blessed art thou, young man, for this good deed. In the day of visitation, God will remember thee.'

"And, indeed, the day of visitation was at hand. King Shedad had now finished building his palace. So he sent out his commands that all his people, men and women, young and old, masters and slaves alike, should come and see his palace, and keep a great feast. On the day appointed they all came. Their tents upon the sands of the desert were as many as the waves of the sea. And the King went up to the top of the highest tower of the palace that he had built, and showed himself. When the people saw him they shouted, 'He is a God! He is a God!'

"Then in the wantonness of his heart he commanded that the Prophet Houd should be brought. He led the man of God through all the courts with their columns of many-coloured marbles, and the rooms shining with gold and jewels. 'Hast thou ever seen such a sight as this?' he said. 'They say that Heaven has made thee wiser than other men. Canst thou then tell the value of these things?' Houd the prophet answered, 'O Shedad, only in the hour of death can a man value such things.'

"But the pride of the King was not one whit abated. 'Hast thou fault to find with the building?'

"The prophet said, 'The walls are weak, for

Azrael, the Angel of Death can enter in.　The building is ill-secured, for the Icy Wind, which nothing that lives can endure, can pierce it.'

" The King's face fell, and his lips were pale with anger.

" Then he led the Prophet to the top of the tower, and pointed to the multitude ; and when they shouted again, ' He is a God!　He is a God!' he asked, ' Say, Prophet, do they not speak the truth ? '

" The Prophet said not a word, but when he looked at that great multitude he wept.　As he looked there went up a great cry of joy.　' The messenger is come!　Kail has returned from Mecca, and he brings back the boon which he sought.'　Then we went out, and looked up to the sky, and there was a deep black cloud over our heads.　All the people looked up and blest the coming rain.　Meanwhile the messenger told his tale to the King.

" ' I went to Mecca, and knelt at the Red Hillock, and prayed to God for rain.　And when I had finished my prayer, I saw three clouds in the sky.　One was white like the clouds that hang over the sky at noon ; and one was red, like the clouds that have caught the last rays of the sun in the evening, and the third was black and heavy with its load of rain. As I looked, there came a voice from Heaven, ' Choose, Kail, one of these three.' So I chose the black cloud that was heavy with rain.'

" ' You chose right,' said the King. And all the people shouted ' Right!' But the Prophet stood up and cried, ' Woe to the children of Ad, for death is gone up into her palaces!' Then he turned to the multitude and said, ' Fly from the wrath to come, ye who would save your souls alive, for strong is the hand that holds the bow, and His arrows err not from their mark!'

" Then a few faithful souls came out from the throng and followed him. But the rest answered him with laughter or with curses. And when he was about to depart with the faithful few, he looked back and his eye fell on me. He called me by my name, ' Aswad!' I heard him and trembled. Again he said, ' Aswad!' and I had almost followed ; but I was afraid of the laughter of my friends, and I stayed, and the opportunity was lost.

"When the Prophet had departed the cloud grew blacker and blacker. At length it opened, but there was no rain there, only the Icy Wind of Death. Thousands and tens of thousands fell all around me, till the King and all his people had perished; and I was left alone. Then there came a voice, 'Aswad, in the day of visitation God hath remembered thee!'

"I tried to go forth from the scene of death. The way was open and I could see no barrier, but there was a chain round the place that I could not pass. Twice I attempted to pass. The third time the Voice said, 'Aswad, be content, and bless the Lord. Repent of thy misdeeds, and when thy soul is prepared, breathe thy wish to die,· and Azrael shall come."

"And here I have lived since that day, I know not for how many ages. I have heard no sound but of the fountain as it rises and falls, and of the tree as it whispers in the wind. My clothing has not grown old, and my sandal is not worn upon my foot. But sinner that I am, I dare not ask to die."

This was the tale that Aswad told. Zeinab

said, "You are blessed, Aswad. The Lord who has saved you from destruction will call you when He sees fit. But oh, that when I wished to die Azrael might come for me! This very hour would I go to Hodeirah and my children!"

As she spoke there was heard the rushing of wings, and Azrael stood beside the three. His face was dark and solemn, and indeed he never smiles, but it was not stern. "Zeinab," he said, "thy prayer is heard. Aswad, thy hour is come." When they heard him speak, they fell upon the ground and blessed the voice. "Me too! me too!" cried Thalaba, "O angel of Death, take me too!"

"Son of Hodeirah," said the angel, "it is not thine hour. Thou art chosen to do the will of Heaven, to avenge thy father's death, and to do the mightiest work that ever was done by man. Live and remember this: "Destiny hath marked thee from mankind." In a moment he was gone. And when Thalaba looked round him, the palace and the gardens had vanished away, and he was alone in the desert.

CHAPTER III.

HOW ABDALDAR THE MAGICIAN SOUGHT FOR
THALABA.

ABDALDAR travelled over all Arabia, searching for Thalaba. From tribe to tribe, from town to town, even from tent to tent he passed. When he rose in the morning the wish to find the lad was the first that came into his mind, and when he lay down to sleep it was the last thing that he thought. Even in his dreams it was with him : many times did he come upon some lad whose look and bearing seemed to be such as the fated youth should have ; but when he had warily applied the ring to him, the fire in the ring still burned, and he knew that he had not finished his search.

At last, when the year was nearly ended, he came to a solitary tent, the cords of which were stretched in a grove of palms. The grove stood in the middle of the desert, like an island in the middle of the sea. There he saw a girl standing under a palm, holding out her apron and looking up to a boy who had climbed into the tree, and was clinging with one arm to the trunk, while with the other he pulled and threw down clusters of dates. Abdaldar approached the tree. He leant upon his staff, and sweat stood upon his forehead. He looked like a venerable old man, somewhat wearied with his day's journey.

"Will it please you to give me some food?" he said.

The girl offered him dates from her lap, and the boy ran to the tent and fetched him a draught of water. Meanwhile the master of the tent, Moath by name, came out and saluted the stranger, and bade them spread a meal for the traveller. They spread it under a Tamarind tree, rice as white as snow, and dates, and figs, and water from the well. The girl also brought water in which she had steeped the acid fruit of the Tamarind. No one who had drunk of this would wish for wine, so refreshing is it. She blushed for joy when

the stranger praised it and drank again.
Meanwhile the boy had fetched a melon. He
had made a hole in the rind days before, and
had closed the wound with wax; and now all
the pulp had been changed into a most delicious
liquid. This he offered to the guest.

Abdaldar ate and was satisfied. And as he
ate he talked of his travels, for he had seen
many countries in his life. Moath sat pleased
to listen to him; and the girl listened as she
took away the dishes, standing with her hands
full to hear what he might next say. But none
listened so eagerly as Thalaba; and to Thalaba
the traveller with seeming kindness chiefly
addressed his talk. With round eyes and open
mouth the boy sat, and, that he might not lose
a word of such delightful talk, came close to
the old man. And he, as if in familiar mood,
laid his hand on Thalaba's arm, and in a
moment the fire out of the ring had fled.

Abdaldar grew pale with joy, for his search
was ended. But at the very moment Moath
said, "It is the hour of prayer. Let us first
make our ablutions, and afterwards praise the
Lord."

The boy fetched water from the well; and they made their ablutions according to the law, and bent their heads to the earth in prayer.

Abdaldar did not bend his head, but stood over Thalaba with his dagger in his hand. But before the arm which he had lifted to strike had the power to descend, the Simoom, the deadly wind of the desert, blew. Moath and Thalaba and the girl, Oneiza, did not feel it, for they were prostrate in prayer; but it smote Abdaldar; and when they rose, they saw the traveller lying dead with the dagger in his hand.

When they were about to bury the Magician, Thalaba spied a ring upon his finger and said, " See, Oneiza, the dead man has a ring! Should it be buried with him ? "

" Surely," she answered, " he was a wicked man, and all that he had was wicked."

" But see how it catches the sunlight and throws it back again. It is a marvellous stone."

" Why do you take it, Thalaba ? Why do you look at it so close ? It may have a charm to blind or poison you. Throw it in the grave. I would not touch it."

" And round its rim are large letters."

"Bury it, bury it."

"It is not written as the Koran is written. Perhaps it is in some other tongue. The accursed man said he had been a traveller."

Meanwhile Moath came out of the tent, and asked, "Thalaba, what have you there?"

"A ring the dead man wore. Perhaps, father, you can read its meaning."

"No, boy; the letters are not such as ours. Heap the sand over it; a wicked man wears nothing holy."

"Nay, do not bury it. Perhaps some traveller may come to our tent who can read it. Or we may find a learned man in some city who can interpret it."

"It were better hid under the sands of the desert. It is likely that this wretched man whom God smote in the very moment of his crime was a Magician, and that these lines are of the language which the demons use. There is, I have heard, a great company of magicians that have their place of meeting in the Domdaniel caverns under the sea."

"And was he who would have killed me one of these?"

" That I do not know. It may be that your
name is written in the book of fate as their
Destroyer, and that God saved your life that
you might do this work."

" Think you that the ring has some strange
power ? "

" Every gem, wise men say, has a power of
its own. Some grow pale or dark and warn
the wearer against poison. Some blunt the
edge of the sword. Some discover hidden
treasures ; and others, again, give us power to
see spirits."

" Father, I will wear this ring."

" Think, Thalaba, what you are doing."

" In the name of God ! if its power be for
good, well ; if for evil, then God and my faith
in Him shall hallow it."

So he put on the ring of gold with the
strange letters written on it. After this they
laid the body of Abdaldar in the grave, and
levelled the dust of the desert over him.

The next day, at sunrise, when Thalaba
went to make his ablutions, he found the grave
open and the body bare. It was not the wind
that had swept away the sand, for the dew lay

undried upon the dust about it. Indeed the night had been so calm and still that not a ripe date had been shaken down from the palms.

When Moath heard the story he said, " I have heard that there are places made so holy by holy men having dwelt in them, that if a dead body should be laid in them they cast him out. It may be that this is such a place. Or can it be that this man is so foul with sorcery and wickedness that heaven and earth alike reject him ? We had best forsake the station. Let us strike our tent. And see there the vulture ! It has already scented its prey. And, indeed, that is the best sepulchre for this accursed one."

Then they purified themselves from the pollution of death. Thalaba drew up the cords of the tent, and Moath furled it, and Oneiza led the camels out of the grove of palms to receive their load. The dew was dried from the ground when they left the Island of palms; when they halted at noon they could see them in the distance, as we see the sails of a fleet far off at sea. At sunset the Island had passed out of their sight. Then they pitched their tent and lay down to sleep.

At midnight Thalaba felt that the ring moved upon his finger. The magicians of the cave knew by their art that he had possessed himself of it, and sent an evil spirit to steal it from him. He called on the name of God, and Moath heard him. "What ails you, Thalaba?" he cried. "Are there robbers in the tent?"

"See you not a spirit in the tent?"

"I see moonlight shining, and I see you standing in it, and I see your shadow, but I see no more."

The lad said no more to Moath, but spoke to the spirit, "Spirit, what brings thee hither? In the name of God, I charge thee to tell me."

"I came for the ring."

"Who was he that slew my father?"

"Okba, the magician, slew him."

"Where does the murderer dwell?"

"In the Domdaniel cavern under the sea."

"Why was my father slain and his children with him?"

"Because we know that the Destroyer was to come of the race of Hodeirah."

" Bring me my father's sword."

" A fire surrounds it. Neither Spirit nor Magician can pierce that fire."

" Bring me his bow and arrows."

Moath and Oneiza, who stood watching from the inner tent, heard Thalaba speak ; but they could not hear the Spirit, for the sound of his voice was too fine for their ears. And now, as they listened, there was a rattle of arrows, and they saw a full quiver laid at the lad's feet, and a bow in his hand. He looked at the bow with joy, and twanged the string. Then he spoke again to the Spirit, " In the name of God, I command thee and all thy fellows never to trouble this tent again."

And from that hour no evil spirit came again to the tent.

CHAPTER IV.

AND now Thalaba lived in peace in Moath's tent four years or so, till he was grown to a man's strength and stature. He could bend his father's bow, nor use his whole strength to do it. He was tall and shapely. Indeed there was not a handsomer or stronger youth in the whole of Arabia. Moath loved him as a son. He had found him years before alone in the wilderness, weeping for his mother, and pitied him. But when he heard his wonderful tale, and saw how his heart was set on a great task that he had to do, his pity was changed into reverence, and he kept the boy with such care as he would have kept a trust from God. Moath loved Thalaba as father loves his son, and Oneiza loved him as a sister loves her brother, and Thalaba loved them both dearly in return. The master of the Tent was neither rich nor poor. God had given him enough and a contented mind. Camels he had which Thalaba tended ; and goats which Oneiza milked. The clothes that they wore were spun by the maid's nimble fingers. So they lived happily, wanting nothing from without.

Nevertheless, in his inmost heart Thalaba was not content, but thought of the work to which he was called, and was impatient to set about it. He would often dream that the time was come, would dream that he had lifted his hand to strike his father's murderer, and that he had his hand upon the sword that was circled with fire.

One day, he and Oneiza were amusing themselves with Hodeirah's bow, for now the girl had strength enough to bend it, and could send an arrow straight up into the air, so far that the eye could scarcely follow its flight. As he looked he said, "When will the hour come for me to use these arrows in avenging my father? Am I not strong enough? or can the will of Heaven be changed, and I am not to be called?"

" Impatient boy," said Moath, smiling.

" Impatient Thalaba!" said Oneiza, smiling also, but somewhat sadly.

Just at that moment there passed over their heads a cloud of locusts, winging their way eastward from Syria.

" See," said Moath, " see how all things obey their doom! They have done their appointed work, eating up the fields of men for their sins, and now they go to their graves. She how the birds follow them, and soar above them, and thin them as they fly, rejoicing in their banquet. Do you think, as some would tell you, that these birds, which we welcome as the destroyers of the locusts, are brought hither by the charms of the priests ? Not so—God sends the locusts to punish man, and He sends also the birds to rid us of them when the time is come."

Meanwhile Oneiza was looking up to where one of the birds was flying above her head. As she looked, he dropped a locust from his talons, and it fell upon her robe. Beautiful was the creature, with its grass-green body and double sets of wings, and its jet-black eyes, and glossy glistening breastplate, as it seemed.

As she looked, she seemed to see mysterious lines upon its forehead. "Look, father! do you know what is here written?" she cried; and to Thalaba, "Look! it may be that these lines are written in the language of the ring."

Thalaba bent down and looked. In a moment his cheeks grew red, and he started back, for these lines could be plainly read, "When the Sun shall be darkened at noon, depart, Son of Hodeirah."

Moath and Oneiza were troubled, but Thalaba rejoiced. Every day at noon he watched the sky. Meanwhile he made new plumes for his arrows, and sharpened their points.

"Are you weary, then, of the tent?" said Moath.

"Not so," said Thalaba, "but I would go and do my work, and return never to leave you any more."

As Thalaba spoke, Oneiza looked again at the sun, and saw, or thought she saw, a speck upon it. It was so small that none who were watching the sun that day had yet perceived it; but Oneiza's eyes were sharpened by love. Certainly it was there; and it grew and grew, and Thalaba put the full quiver on his shoulder, and took the bow in his hand, and prepared to depart. And now half the Sun is covered, and now, again, the day grows dark, and the birds go to roost, and the owl, the bird of night, comes forth, and the eyes of the Hyæna are seen to glare.

"Farewell, my father! farewell, Oneiza!" said Thalaba.

"Will you not wait for a sign to show the way?" said Moath.

"God will conduct me," said Thalaba, and went out into the darkness, and they heard his steps as he went, and the quiver rattling on his shoulders.

He had not gone far when he saw a dim shape in the darkness. As he looked it grew brighter, and he recognized the form and face of his mother. "Go," she said, "to Babylon, and ask the Angels for the talisman."

The spirit came towards him as it spake, as though to give him a mother's kiss, and Thalaba ran forward. But all that he felt was the wind playing on his cheek, and all that he saw was the darkness. "Mother, mother!" he cried, "let me see you again."

"You shall see me," she said, "in the hour of death."

Then the day dawned again, and the darkness dispersed. Thalaba went on full of hope, and of the expectation of great deeds, and of how he should come back some day to Moath's tent, and of all his thoughts Oneiza was a part. At sunset he came to a well, over which hung an Acacia tree. Then he made his ablutions, and said his prayers, and then brought out his provision of food. As he ate, came a traveller on a camel, who greeted him courteously, and sat down beside him by the well, and kept him company over his meal. The stranger was an old man, but vigorous, and one who scarcely seemed to need the staff which he carried. His eyes were quick and piercing, and his beard long and curly. He was courteous in manner, and his talk ready, and full of knowledge. A traveller could scarce have a more pleasant companion on his way.

As they talked, Thalaba asked, " Whither are you bent ? "

" I go to Bagdad," said the old man.

Thalaba's eyes kindled with joy to hear the word.

"And I too," he said. "May I be your companion?"

"Willingly," said the other.

Then they talked further together.

"You are young to travel."

"I have never yet come beyond the desert."

"We are bound for a noble city; you will see splendid palaces and mosques and rich bazaars, to which merchants bring all the wealth of the world."

"Is it not Bagdad near the site of ancient Babylon?"

"Even so, a long day's journey."

"And the ruins?"

"There is a mighty mass of them; enough to tell us how great were our fathers in comparison of us."

"Do not the angels Haruth and Maruth atone for their sin at Babylon?"

"There is a tale that they do. But Ignorance believes many falsehoods for truth. What have you heard of these same angels?"

"This. Once on a time the angels, talking in heaven, expressed their wonder at the obstinacy of man, that though signs and tokens were given to him, and prophets sent to exhort him, nevertheless he would not repent. So stubborn a creature, they said, should have mercy refused to him for ever. God heard their unforgiving pride, and commanded two of those spirits that had not fallen, because they had not been tempted, to descend to the earth, and judge men's causes. For a time they judged righteously, but when an exceedingly beautiful woman came before 'them, they were tempted. 'Tell me,' said the woman, 'the name of God.' So they told her; and in a moment, by the power of that name, she was lifted up to heaven, and accused them before the judgment seat of God. They were called, but had no defence; only they entreated that the punishment of their sin might not endure for ever, but might at the last restore them purified to their place in heaven. This is the tale that I have heard."

"And you have heard also, doubtless, that the place of their punishment is at Babylon, and that there magicians seek them, and force from their unwilling lips the secrets of sorcery."

" Is not this true ? "

" Have you never seen some familiar shape distorted in the twilight into something uncouth and strange."

" Often ? "

" Just so common things viewed through the mist of error terrify men's minds."

" But is it written in the Book that Haruth and Maruth were thus condemned ? "

" God often teaches us by fables."

" But is not the place of their punishment at Babylon ? "

" Yes, at Babylon they are to be found. But enough for the present. Night is at hand. I am an old man, and my eyes are heavy. We shall have time enough to talk to-morrow. Peace be with you, my son."

CHAPTER V.

THE old traveller wrapped his cloak round him, and lay down to sleep. Thalaba also laid himself down. For a while he watched the moon shining through the leaves of the acacia; then fell asleep. As for his companion, he only seemed to sleep, for indeed he was the Magician Lobaba, who had come from the Domdaniel caverns to slay, if it might be possible, the Destroyer. When he knew from the youth's long and regular breathing that he slept, he rose stealthily from his place, and bending over him looked closely at him. Deeply in his heart he cursed Abdaldar's ring that kept him safe. It was to be seen on Thalaba's finger as he lay with his head on his arm, and the light of the moon was reflected from the gem. Lobaba put out his hand, trying to take it, but could not ; he called the fiends that served him, and bade them rob the sleeping youth. But they were powerless, one and all. And at last the Sorcerer, baffled and full of rage, lay down again. Force could not help him, but he might prevail by temptation.

The morning sunshine fell upon Thalaba's eyes, and woke him. He rose, and folded his mantle round him, and after ablutions duly made and prayers duly said, girded his loins for the day's journey. So did the Magician also, insulting God with the vain show of worship. Then they filled their water-skins at the spring, and gave the camel a full draught, and went on their way.

"Is it true," said Thalaba, "that magicians go to learn the secrets of their wicked art from the angels at Babylon ? "

" It is true and it is false."

" What do you mean ? "

" All things have a double use. The fire that warms us on the hearth may burn the house ; the sun ripens the harvest and darts fever into our veins ; and the iron that the hunter uses may arm the hand of a murderer."

"What then?"

"Nothing is good or evil in itself, but only in its use. All men hold the physician in honour, but there are some who use their skill to poison the cup which a friend drinks; but is his knowledge therefore evil?"

"It were folly to think so."

"O what a noble creature were man, if he knew his own powers and gave them room to grow and spread! The Horse obeys his will; the Camel carries him across the deserts; the Pigeon bears his messages. He is content with these conquests, when he might have myriads of Spirits obey him."

"But how? only surely by making that covenant with Hell which binds the soul to death."

"Was Solomon then accursed of God? Did not the birds make a canopy over him with their wings when he bade them? Did not the Genii build the Temple for him?"

"God gave him his wisdom as a special reward for his goodness."

"Aye, and God will always give wisdom as the reward of study. 'Tis a well of which all might drink ; but few dig deep enough. Whatever powers God has made it possible for man to reach, it is lawful for him to attain, if he can. The knowledge that it does not befit him to have, has been placed beyond his reach. Those who go to Babylon, and learn mysterious wisdom from the angels, do no wrong."

" Do you know any of their secrets ? "

" Alas ! my son, I know but enough to see how great is my ignorance. My age has been given to study, but I can only regret in vain the careless indolence of my youth. Yet something I know of the properties of herbs, and have often brought comfort to the afflicted by my art, blessed by Him without whose blessing nothing avails. Also of gems I know something."

" Can you interpret what is written round this ring ? "

" My sight is weak, let me see it closer."

The unsuspecting Thalaba was about to draw the ring from his finger, when a wasp settled on the joint above the ring, and stung it. The flesh rose hot and purple round the ring ; and the Magician, baffled again, knew the hand of

Heaven, and blasphemed in his heart. Then he devised another scheme. At noon there rose a mist. For a time the Sun guided them on their way, and it was pleasant to travel without the heat. But this guidance soon failed them. An impenetrable mass of cloud hung over the wilderness.

"Do you know the track?" said Thalaba, "or shall we wait till the wind scatters this fog?"

"Let us hold on," said the Magician. "If we go astray, the Sun will set us right to-morrow."

So they went deeper and deeper into the wilderness. That night they lay down to sleep in the darkness, and the next morning when Thalaba awoke he did not know which way to turn for his prayers.

"Shall we go on," said Lobaba, "or shall we wait? If we go, we may lose ourselves yet worse; if we wait, food and drink may fail us."

"Let us go," answered Thalaba; "we may find, it may be, some tent or grove of palms. To wait were to wait for death."

And willingly the Magician led the youth

still deeper into the desert. The mist hung over it still; it was there at night when they lay down to sleep; it was there as thick as ever when they awoke in the morning. And now the water-skin was light, though they used its precious contents with prudence. During the third night, as Thalaba lay in a broken sleep, he heard in his dreams the sound of rushing winds; but when he awoke, there was still the same deadly calm. So another day passed, and now the water-skin was empty.

Then the travellers heard a hopeful sound, the sound of the wind. In a few minutes the mist was scattered, and they saw again the face of heaven. But what a scene it was on which they opened their eyes! No well was near, no palm grove, no tent. The skin lay flat on the camel, and the poor beast could scarcely drag his weary feet across the sand.

At the height of their despair there burst upon their eyes a beautiful sight, a green meadow spangled with flowers. Surely a stream must flow through it. The Camel saw it, and hurried on with fresh spirit. But when they reached the place, they found that the flowers were nothing better than the bitter herbs of gentian and senna. Lobaba said, "Son, we must slay the camel, or we shall perish. Your young hand is strong and firm ; draw forth your knife and pierce him."

No one who saw the old man with suffering face, dry lips, and feverish eyes, would have dreamt that in truth he felt no pain or distress, such was the strength of his magic. Thalaba paused for a moment; but when he saw his companion's distress, and saw the poor beast lie at his feet worn out with want, he did not hesitate any more, but taking the knife from his girdle drew it across the camel's throat. "Little will your death profit us," he thought, as he poured into their water-skin the scanty portion that was hoarded in the camel's stomach. For a day it lasted them. Then it was exhausted, and still there was no cloud nor hope of rain.

Lobaba said, "Let me look at the Ring." So he took the youth's hand and viewed the writing close. "Joy!" he cried, " whosoever bears this stone may command the Genii. Call them, my son ; bid them save us."

"No," said Thalaba, "shall I distrust my God? If He will not save us, the Genii cannot help."

Whilst he was speaking, Lobaba's eyes were fixed on the distance with such terror in them that Thalaba looked to see what it might mean. He saw columns of sand burning red with the sun upon them, rushing before the wind and coming towards them. As they looked the foremost of them burst, scattering the burning sand about it.

"Save us!" cried the Magician, "save us by the Ring!"

Thalaba made no answer, but gazed wondering and awestruck on the sight.

"Why do you wait?" cried the old man. "If God will not save, call on the Powers that will."

"Ah!" said Thalaba, "now I know you, accursed sorcerer; you have led me hither, hoping that for fear of death I should sell my soul to sin."

"Fool! call on him whose name is written on the Ring or die!"

"Die thou." And as he spoke he put an

arrow on the bowstring, and drew the bow to the full, and let fly. The arrow sped true to its aim, smiting the Sorcerer full upon the breast, but the astonished Thalaba saw the point recoil blunted.

Lobaba smiled bitterly. " Try again your earthly arms. The Power I serve does not desert his votaries as He does whom you worship."

As he spoke, he called by his magic art a chariot of the air, that moved of its own power. On this he climbed, and cried to Thalaba, " Come hither; you have been my fellow-traveller, and I am yet willing to save you. Mount this chariot and you are safe."

Thalaba did not deign to answer him. But as he looked, another of the great columns of sand came eddying across the desert. It struck Lobaba as he sat in his chariot, and laid him a corpse upon the ground; but over Thalaba, who had thrown himself with his face to the earth, it passed harmless.

CHAPTER VI.

THALABA rose from the earth, and bent his head
in prayer. When he lifted it up, the sky was
overcast with clouds, which before long came
down in rain. He bared his head, and stretched
his hands to the shower, and felt refreshed. As
he did this he heard a loud, quick panting, and
looking up saw a tiger run by, its head hanging
low, its dry tongue lolling out of its mouth.
Thalaba knew that the beast was searching for
water, and following it at a distance saw it
stoop down and drink. A pelican had built its
nest in the wilderness, and had carried thither
a stock of water for its young, which were
swimming and dipping their heads in the bath.
When the tiger approached, they crowded
nestling under their mother's wings ; the beast
drank, but did not harm them. Of the tiger the

mother bird had no fear, for it was a familiar guest. But when the man came near she menaced him with her wings and outstretched neck, emboldened by a mother's terrors. Thalaba drank and filled his water-skin, yet left enough for life to the pelican and her young. Then as he departed he blessed the carrier-bird, the dweller in the desert, and Him, the Common Father, who provides for all His creatures, and so went with new strength and confidence on his way.

After many a day's toil he came to Bagdad. There indeed, for all its pomp and wealth, though the merchants of East and West met in her bazaars, and long troops of laden camels lined her streets, and Tigris bore fleets of vessels on his stream, Thalaba did not linger for a day. He loathed everything that should delay the hour, when returning from his search, he should hang Hodeirah's sword on the pillar of Moath's tent. Before the sun had risen he passed out of the gates, and the last light of the sun was in the horizon when he came to the ruins of Babylon. It was a desolate place; the scorpion basked in the palace courts, and the she-wolf hid her litter in the temples. The Arab never pitched his tent within the walls, and the shepherd drove his flocks far from them. And Thalaba went cautiously, feeling the ground before him with his bow, till he came to a place where he could proceed no longer, the ruins closing him in on every side. He leant against a broken column, thinking what he should next do. Soon he heard steps approaching, and turning saw in the moonlight a man in full armour approaching.

"Who are you," said the stranger, "that at such an hour you wander in such a place as this? A traveller that has lost his way? or a robber hiding his plunder, or a magician with spells to make these ruins disclose the treasures that some say are buried among them?"

"I am neither traveller, nor robber, nor magician," said Thalaba; "I seek the angels, Haruth and Maruth; but tell me, Stranger, why are you here?"

The soldier, himself haughty and fearless, was not ill-pleased with the lad's spirit. "Do you know," he said, "the cause of their punishment?"

" I have been seeking for it in vain."

" Have you courage to tread a dangerous path ? "

" Lead on !"

" Young Arab, if your heart beats evenly in danger ; if you do not fear what makes other men tremble ; if you can look undismayed at what even the soldier well tried in battle might well shrink from, then follow me, for I am bound for the cave."

" Lead on," said Thalaba again, and Mohareb (for that was the stranger's name) led the way.

There was a strange sound about the two as they went. It was not the wind, for Thalaba's long locks lay unmoved upon his shoulders. It was not the roar of the river as it rushed down some waterfall, for Euphrates flowed quietly over the plain. It came from the black boiling springs that rose in the great bitumen lake. Along the lake's side the two travellers walked, till they came to a cave out of the mouth of which the black torrent rolled. Mohareb turned to Thalaba and said, " Dare you enter it ? "

" Lead on," said Thalaba the third time, and set his foot inside the cave.

" Stay, madman!" cried his guide, " would you rush headlong on certain death ? Where are your arms with which to meet the Keeper of the passage ? "

A loud shriek from the depths of the cavern drowned Thalaba's answer. " Fate favours you," said Mohareb, " or your name had been blotted to-day out of the Book of Life."

As he spoke he drew a bag from underneath his cloak. " You are a brave boy," he said, " but to leap unprepared into danger, as lions rush upon the hunter's spear, is folly. Zohak the giant keeps the passage, and it is not by force we can win it." He drew a man's hand, shrivelled and dry and black, out of the bag, and fitted a taper into the fingers. " See," said he, " this is a murderer's hand ; the very hand with which he did the deed. I drove the vultures from the stake on which he died impaled, and cut off the hand, and dried it for nine weeks in the sun. And the taper—but you have not learnt these secrets. See how clear it burns, but its ingredients scatter a deathly vapour through the cave; and when the keeper of the passage feels them, it will lull even his agony to sleep, and he will leave the passage free."

Mohareb led the way with the taper in his hand; and now they came to where the cave became loftier and narrower. Here Zohak sat with great snakes growing from his shoulders. Mohareb held the taper towards him; and the magic spell of the taper had such power that his eyes closed in sleep, and he lay all his length along the floor of the passage. But the two snakes were not asleep. They darted out their fiery tongues, and shut the passage. Mohareb drew from his wallet two fresh human heads, and threw them down before them. They turned eagerly to their horrid feast, and the travellers passed unharmed. And now the cave opened wider than before, till they came to a great pit, so deep and black that no eye could pierce its darkness.

"Here," said Mohareb, "the angels that teach enchantments dwell."

Thalaba said aloud, "Haruth and Maruth, hear us! I do not come to learn forbidden secrets. By God's command I am here. Tell me the Talisman."

"Do you think," said Mohareb, "that you will thus trick them out of their secret? Keep this righteousness of the lip for the mosque and the market-place. The spirits know the heart; only compelled by strong and torturing spells will they tell you the secret by which you can descend."

"Descend!" cried Thalaba, astonished.

"What!" said Mohareb, "have I led some silly prayermonger here? What brings you to this place? By heaven you shall pay for your folly in coming." And he lifted his scymitar to strike him.

He lifted it; but his arm hung powerless in the air; for the mighty spell of the Ring forbad it to fall. In a rage he cried, "Then this is your trust in God! He had failed to save you but for the Ring. It is to spells and magic that you trust after all."

"Blasphemer!" cried Thalaba, "do you say that I trust in magic spells for want of faith in God? See now." And he took Abdaldar's ring from his finger, and threw it into the pit.

A skinny hand came up, and caught it as it fell, and peals of devilish laughter shook the cave.

Mohareb's cheek flushed with joy, and he lifted his scymitar again. Thalaba saw the blue gleam of the blade as it descended, and sprang at the soldier, and grappled him breast to breast. Mohareb was sinewy and large of limb, broad shouldered, and his joints well knit, and he was practised in the art of war. Thalaba's strength was not so mature ; but the inspiration of the moment gave him the strength of a madman. Mohareb reeled before him. With knee and breast and arm he pressed on his enemy and drove him backwards to the very brink of the pit. For a moment they struggled fiercely on the very edge ; then with a fresh impulse of force Thalaba thrust him down, and Mohareb was engulfed in the abyss.

His breath came fast with the struggle. Panting he breathed out a broken prayer of thankfulness ; then said—

" Haruth and Maruth, are ye here ? or has that servant of sin misled me ? I, Thalaba, Servant of the Lord, invoke you. Hear me ; so may Heaven accept your penitence. I go to root out of earth the sorcerer brood. Tell me the Talisman I need."

As he spoke, beyond the abyss he saw the angels reclining on the rock. Their faces were sad; but guilt and shame had been purged away. This was their answer. "Son of Hodeirah! thou hast proved it here. The Talisman is Faith."

CHAPTER VII.

THE PARADISE OF SIN.

THALABA retraced his steps to the outer air. The giant Zohak lay stretched on the ground. He was awake indeed, but he did not reach out his hand to bar the way, fearing to rouse the snakes, which were still lingering over their meal. Gladly Thalaba found himself at last again in the outer air, and gladly he lay down to sleep in the shelter of a ruin of which the roof was yet left.

The next morning when he awoke, he found a horse standing by his side. Never had he seen one of more faultless shape and brighter eye ; no not even among those that are said to come from King Solomon's own stud. He was adorned with rich trappings of crimson, but had neither bit nor bridle in his mouth.

"Surely," said Thalaba to himself, "he is sent by Heaven, and will go as Heaven bids him. It is not the rider who is to guide him." Meanwhile the creature threw up his head, and pawed the ground as if impatient to start. So Thalaba leapt lightly on his back, and in a moment the horse bounded away. Over the plain he sped, and did not halt till the sun was low in the sky. Then he paused; Thalaba lay down to sleep, and the horse rested by his side. So they travelled on day after day, till one evening, when they halted, the horse sprang away. He had done his errand. The evening was dark, the clouds hiding the moon; nor could Thalaba hear any sound but of running water; guiding his way by this, he came to a little stream, one of many with which the ground was intersected. The first from which he stooped to drink was boiling hot; but the steam rising from his hand warned him in time not to try it. The next was intensely cold. Of this he drank deeply, and thus refreshed lay down to sleep.

The next day, following the rills, he came to a river into which they flowed. There looking

about him he saw in the distance a high range
of mountains, and, leading up to them, a wide
stony valley. Something seemed to tell him
that this was the path which he must follow.
As he went on, still mounting higher and
higher, the valley grew narrower, and the
rocks steeper on either side, till at last he
came to a place where they met, barring all
further passage; in the barrier indeed there
had been hewn an opening, but this was
closed by massive gates of iron. A horn with
ivory tip and mouth of brass hung by the
gates. This Thalaba took, and breathed into
the mouth. The blast rang like thunder
among the rocks; and the gates rolled back
without any one to move them. He entered,
and they closed behind him with a clap like
thunder. It was a narrow winding way in
which he found himself, lighted by dim lamps
that hung from the roof, and descended con-
tinually. At last Thalaba found his way
barred again by gates of iron, but by these
latter also hung a horn of brass and ivory.
Thalaba took it and breathed into it. This
time the answer came not in thunder, but in

the sweetest music that can be imagined.
And again the gates rolled back of their own
accord. For a moment Thalaba thought he
must be in the very garden of Eden. But
Eden had no marble terraces, nor tents of
cloth of gold, such as could be seen among
the perfumed groves and shrubberies of this
wonderful place. And then he thought that
he must be dreaming, and shut his eyes, but
when he opened them again everything was
there, palaces and glittering courts and perfumed groves. As he looked and wondered,
an old man of a very gracious and reverend
look came forward and greeted him. "Happy
youth, go and taste the joys of Paradise.
The reinless horse that ranges over the
world brings hither only those that are
marked out for great deeds. Here they have
a foretaste of happiness; hence they go out
bound on great enterprises; hither they return to an endless felicity. Go then and
taste the joys of Paradise."

He turned away and left the youth silent
with wonder. Wherever his eyes could reach
he saw new marvels of delight. Through

openings in the woods he saw rich pavilions curtained with gold. Streams clear as crystal wandered through the shrubbery and lawn. The broad-leaved planes arched over in long colonnades, while round their trunks the vines climbed up, clothing them with a yet fresher green and with clusters of purple and gold. And the ground was carpeted with flowers, tulips streaked with the sky at sunset, and the lily with her snowy head and the red-bosomed rose. The air, too, was full of music, while the nightingale sang from his bower of roses more sweetly than he ever sang on earth, and from far away came the cries of the waterfowls, and now and then, mellowed by the distance, came the voice of merriment. Thalaba wandered on, till at length, at the bidding of hunger, he entered a banqueting-room. There on the brink of a fountain, on carpets of silk, sat a company of guests. The air was cooled by the water as it rose and fell ; the very light came cooled through panes of pearly shell, or was tinged saffron or ruby as it fell through vases of wine that filled the openings in the ceiling. In that delicious coolness the re-

vellers reclined at ease, and drank from
goblets of gold the amber juice of the grapes
of Shiraz. Thalaba would have none of the
wine, knowing it to be forbidden, and indeed
the mother of sins ; nor did the guests offer
it a second time, for they saw that this youth
was not one who could be turned from his
purpose. But he drank the water, water that
seemed clearer and purer than when it came
from the spring ; and partook of the fruits,
for there were fruits of all kinds, water-melons
with rough rinds that melted on the lips, and
pistachio nuts, and amber grapes from Persia
that had been dried in the sun till they were
all sweetness, and apricots cased in ice, like
topazes set in crystal, and oranges on plates
of snow. And as he ate, the rich smoke from
aloes and sandalwood burning in censers of
gold filled the room with perfume. Then came
in a troop of dancers, with bells upon their
ankles, and danced before the guests, making
music as they moved. But Thalaba rose dis-
pleased, thinking that it did not become the
lover of Oneiza to be in such company, and
leaving the banqueting-room wandered forth

into the garden. As he looked, he could not but remember that he was a lonely man, wandering about the world, and shut out from the joys of home, and for a moment he murmured against the will of Heaven.

Hurrying away from those scenes of revelry, he sought the shade and silence of the wood, and there throwing himself on the ground thought of the desert and of Moath's tent and of Oneiza. As he dreamed he was roused by a cry of distress. It came louder and nearer, and he started up, strung his bow, and plucked an arrow from the quiver. He heard the cry again, and now it was close at hand; and it was a woman's shriek. In another moment he saw a woman rush through the trees, her veil half torn from her face, and her pursuer close behind. " Help me," she cried, turning to Thalaba. At the word the arrow flew, and did its errand of death. Then he turned to the woman and saw—Oneiza.

When she could breathe again she cried, "O my father! my father!" Thalaba lost in wonder and fearing to ask could but wait with her. " They seized me, Thalaba," she said,

Dancing Girls.

" they seized me in my sleep at night. My father could not help me; he is an old man, and they were many and strong. To think that they could have heard his prayer and yet leave him childless!"

" We will seek him; we will go back to the desert."

"Alas! we should not find him. Our tent is desolate. The wind has heaped the sand within the door. My father wanders about the world seeking me. O Thalaba, this is a wicked place; let us be gone."

" But how? How shall we pass the iron gates? They moved at a breath to let me in, but armies could not stir them for my return."

"We will climb the mountains that shut in this hateful garden."

" Are you strong enough to climb?"

" Strong enough surely for anything, partly from fear, and partly, dear Thalaba, that you are with me."

As she spoke she took his hand, and drew him gently towards the mountains. But when they came to the foot of them, they found no slopes gradually leading upward, but steep cliffs, rising sheer from the ground. There was no way by which the most skilful and bold of mountaineers could climb.

"There is no way," said Thalaba, and Oneiza grew pale and her steps flagged. "But stay," said the youth, "I passed a river, a full stream; the waters cannot be kept in, and where they find a way it may be that we can follow. This way the river runs."

They followed the course of the stream, as it rolled along full and silent; but as they advanced they heard a sound as of a waterfall louder and louder, and so came to a place where the whole plunged at one leap down a precipice of rock.

"God save us!" cried Oneiza; "there is no way from this accursed place," and her heart sank with fear.

"Cheer up," Thalaba said; "if we cannot escape the dangers of this place, yet we can conquer them. But tell me who has prepared this garden of delights and for what?"

"When I was brought here," answered Oneiza, "the women told me that it was the abode of the magician Aloaddin. He intoxicates men with the delights of this place, till they are ready to commit all manner of crimes at his bidding. And what will you do against all these?"

Thalaba's face grew dark as he heard. "Woe to him," he said, with a stern smile, "woe to him! he laid a net for an Antelope, but a Lion has come in."

She shook her head. "Ah! but he is a sorcerer, and guarded by many; and you, Thalaba, are but one."

"Ay, but there is a God, Oneiza, and I have a Talisman that protects from all the powers of Earth and Hell whoever bears it. Remember, too, that Destiny has marked me from mankind. But now lie down and rest, fearing no evil. I will watch by you."

So Oneiza lay down on a bank of flowers; and after she had calmed her spirit with prayer, sank peacefully to sleep. And Thalaba sat and watched her, and as he watched his spirit rose, and he waited in good hope for the day.

CHAPTER VIII.

HOW ONEIZA WAS SAVED AND LOST.

THE song of the lark awoke Oneiza, and she wished, as she watched the bird twinkling in the morning light, that she had wings and liberty like him. Her cheek flushed and grew pale again, but Thalaba was calm and ready for his work. But first he considered how he should arm himself, remembering that his arrow had fallen with a blunted point from Lobaba's breast. It might well be, he thought, that Aloaddin might be protected by a spell of equal power. Thus thinking he caught sight of a young poplar that stood by the brink of the river, with its leaves shivering in the wind, and turned to Oneiza and said, " I remember how in the old days you would bring down the clusters of dates from the palms, cutting the stalks with the arrow, so true was your aim. Take the bow again, dear maid ; I must have different arms."

So speaking he grasped the poplar with both hands, and wrenched it from the earth, roots and all. From these he shook off the clotted earth, and broke away the head, and boughs, and lesser roots, till he had fashioned a mighty club. "Now I am ready for this child of sin. He shall exchange, maybe to-day, his paradise for a far different dwelling."

So the youth and the maid went to the centre of the garden. It so chanced that Aloaddin had that day assembled all the inhabitants, and the two mingled unnoticed with the throng, or if any one noticed them it was to say, "See a daughter of the Homerites who remembers yet the tents of the tribes, for their women know how to wield the bow and the spear." "Nay," his neighbour would answer, "it is a love pageant. He with that fierce eye and massy club mimics some lion-tamer, and she plays the heroine with her arrows and her bow."

Aloaddin sat on a throne of gold, his crown and robe shining with jewels. Over his head hovered a huge bird, so huge that an eagle would have been but like a sparrow in his clasp. His breast was iron and his feathers burnished gold, and he waved his wings, at once a canopy and a fan. The crowd bent their knees to the sorcerer, and shouted, " Hail, great Giver of Joy, Lord of Paradise !" Then he rose to speak, and they stood silent.

" Children of Earth, the Infidel Sultan, whose lands are bordered by my mountains, threatens me. He has strong armies and many guards ; yet a dagger may find him. I do not tempt you with vain stories of a heaven from which no one has returned. You have tasted of happiness here. Who will earn it for ever for himself by a deed of danger ?"

" I will," cried Thalaba, and leaping forward dashed his mighty club on the Sorcerer's head. The wretch fell, for his skull was shattered, but some charm still kept his life imprisoned in his body. The crowd stood astonished, waiting to see the vengeance of Heaven fall on Thalaba. And indeed the Monster Bird pounced down to seize him. But before he could strike with his beak, Oneiza let fly an arrow from the mighty bow with so true an aim that it pierced the creature to the heart. With that the Talisman was broken; and while the earth shook and the heavens thundered, the Paradise of Sin vanished away. Now too the mountains that had by magic enclosed the place were rent, and Thalaba and Oneiza, left alone in the midst of desolation and death, went down the rocky glen into the valley below.

In the valley the Sultan had pitched his camp. As he sat in his tent in council with his chiefs, Thalaba and the maid were brought before him by a captain who thus told his tale.

"As we passed towards the mountains in obedience to your command, suddenly the earth shook, and the air became dark as mid-night, and the lightnings flashed, and the thunders rolled round us. It seemed as if the very judgment-day had come. When we ventured to proceed there met us this youth and maid who told us that they were come from Aloaddin's halls, that the judgment-stroke had fallen upon him, and that he and his Paradise of Sin were destroyed. We brought them here that they might repeat the tale in your presence."

"If thou hast lied," said the Sultan to the youth, " thou shalt die.   If thou speakest truth, thou shalt stand next to myself."

" Be it done to me," answered Thalaba, " as the truth shall prove."

While he was speaking, a great cry was heard, and a messenger flew breathless and panting into the tent.   " O King, live for ever!" he said.   " May all thy foes be as Aloaddin, for God has smitten him."

The Sultan cried, " Put the robe of honour on the Arabian, and put a chain of gold around his neck, and my crown on his head, and set him on my horse of state, and lead him through the camp, and let the heralds go before him and cry, 'Thus shall it be done to the man whom the King honours.' "

So they put the robe of honour on Thalaba, and a chain of gold about his neck, and the King's crown on his head, and led him through the camp on the King's own horse, and the heralds cried before him as the King had commanded.

When Thalaba had come from the presence of the King, he sought Oneiza and said, " The

King has done as he said. I am next to himself in this land. But why so sad? When I
heard of these honours, my thought was at
once of you, that you also would be happy."

" But, Thalaba, am not I an orphan and
among strangers?"

" But with me."

" But think, Thalaba—my father!"

" Nay, take comfort. Remember in what
danger we were this morning, and now we have
safety and honour and wealth. The Sultan
asked me about you but just now. I told him
that we had been plighted from childhood.
Was I wrong, Oneiza? He said that he
would heap our marriage with gifts. But
why these tears?"

" *Remember Destiny hath marked thee from
mankind.*"

" Perhaps the mission ceased when Aloaddin
perished, or if not, why should I not abide in
peace till I am called?"

" Take me to the desert."

" Moath is not there. Would you dwell in a
stranger's tent?"

" Take me to Mecca. Let me be a servant.

of the Temple. Bind my veil with your own hand. It shall never be lifted again, and I will pray for your success."

"Nay, Oneiza, think of better things. Report will soon spread about the fame of these events, and your father will hear, and join us. Only consent to be my wife."

So Oneiza, overborne by his entreaties, and following her own heart, consented.

With song and music and dance the bridal procession went carrying Oneiza to her husband's house. Behind the bride went fifty women in robes woven with thread of gold; and behind them again came a hundred slaves bearing vessels of gold and silver and splendid apparel, the Sultan's marriage gifts. On either hand the pages carried the torches glowing in the darkness; and the trumpets and timbrels made music, and the multitudes shouted, till they came to the palace of Thalaba, where the marriage feast was spread.

But when the feast was finished and the guests had departed,—who is this that comes from the bridal chamber? It is Azrael, the Angel of Death——

CHAPTER IX.

MEANWHILE Moath, searching for his daughter, had come to the Sultan's city, and wandering outside the walls found the burial ground. A woman met him and said, "Old man, go not among the tombs. There is a madman there."

"Will he harm me, think you?"

"Not he, poor wretch. But 'tis a most miserable thing to see his grief. All day and all night long he lies upon a grave; he never weeps or groans; never opens his lips even to pray. I have taken him food for charity's sake, but he never thanked me. I say, go not among the tombs, old man."

"But say, why has God so smitten him?"

"He came to this country a stranger, and did some great service to the Sultan, who therefore named him next to himself, and gave him a palace, and dowered his bride with houses and lands. But on his wedding day the Angel of Death came for his bride. He never leaves her grave. When the Sultan heard the tale, he said that doubtless Heaven had smitten him for some secret wickedness, and prayed forgiveness that he had shown him any favour, and so left him to perish."

"Did you say that he was a stranger?"

"Yes, an Arab like you. But I say, go not among the tombs; you will see such a sight as you will never forget."

"Nay, I have never shunned a countryman in distress, and the sound of his native tongue, maybe, will calm him as the voice of a friend."

Then the woman pointed the way to the sepulchre, and Moath, going as she bid him, found Thalaba lying on the grave. His raven black hair was rusted with sun and rain, and his cheeks had fallen. As he lay, his fingers played unwittingly with the grass upon the grave. Moath did not know him, so much changed was he, but drawing near said, "Peace be with you." The sound of his native tongue roused Thalaba, but when he looked up and saw the good old man, he rose and fell upon his neck, and groaned. Then Moath knew him, and a dreadful fear came over him that he was childless. He said nothing, but pointed to the tomb. " Yes," said Thalaba, as if he had spoken—" yes, your search is ended here."

The father's cheeks grew pale, and his lips quivered with grief. Still he could say, " God is good! His will be done!"

It softened Thalaba to see such grief and such resignation. " Ah," said he, " you have a comforter in your trouble. But in me, Moath, you see a wretch whom God has abandoned;" and then, when the old man looked at him incredulous—" nightly," he went on, " Oneiza comes to drive me to despair. You think me mad. But dare you come and see her when the crier proclaims midnight from the minaret-top?"

And now the sun was about to set, and Moath, as he saw the white flag waving on the mosque, said, " Thalaba, do you not pray?"

" I must not pray," said he, with such a groan as went to the old man's heart and made him bow down and in a fervent agony pray to God.

It was a wet and stormy night, and Thalaba led the old man into the chamber of the Tomb to shelter him from the rain. They heard the storm beat on the monument above ; and there on Oneiza's grave, the two sat, her father and her husband. The crier proclaimed midnight from the minaret-top.

"Now, now!" cried Thalaba, and as he spoke, there spread a lurid light over the tomb, and Oneiza stood before them, a corpse, and yet with a brightness in her eye more terrible than death.

"What! art thou still living, wretch?" she cried. "Must I leave my couch every night, to tell thee that God has abandoned thee?"

"This is not Oneiza," cried the old man ; "it is a fiend, a manifest fiend," and he held his lance to the youth. "Strike her! strike her!"

"What? strike *her*," said Thalaba, and stood paralysed, gazing on the dreadful form.

"Yes, strike her," cried another voice ; and while Thalaba turned round to see whence it came, Moath performed its bidding, and thrust his lance. The fiend fled howling with the wound ; and in a moment, clad in a golden light, the true Oneiza stood before them.

"Oh, Thalaba!" she cried, "abandon not thyself—go on, finish thy work, that in Paradise I may not wait for thee long." Then she turned to Moath, "Thy way is short to Paradise, dear father. Return to the Desert. Azrael the Deliverer will soon come for you."

Then the Spirit vanished from their sight, and the darkness closed round them again. Thalaba took his bow and quiver from the ground.

"Thank God," he said, "that in my madness I did not forget these. To-morrow I will brace it afresh in the sun. And I, like the bow, will brace myself for the work that lies before me. And now, dear father, we part, not to meet again till we meet in Paradise."

Moath made no answer, but followed him to the door of the Tomb chamber. The rain had ceased, and the clouds were carried wildly by the wind across the sky ; and it chanced that in one of the rifts before them a star shot eastward, leaving a path of light behind it.

"See, my guide," said Thalaba; and the old man blessed him. So they parted, and Thalaba went his way.

That evening a Dervish, sitting in the sun at the door of his cell, invited the youth to stay with him for the night, and spread before him his simple meal, rice and fresh grapes and water from the brook. As they sat and talked, a wedding procession went by with singing and music and dancing. The Dervish gave them his blessing as they went by, but Thalaba hid his face in his hands and groaned. Now the old man had himself known sorrow, and he felt pity for the youth, and Thalaba, comforted by his words, told him all his trouble.

"My son," said he, "it is God that has chastened you. See this vine. When I found it, it was wasting its strength in luxuriant growth and gave no fruit; but I pruned it, and see what beautiful clusters it has supplied. It is thus Heaven deals with us; but say, whither are you going?"

"I go straight on," said Thalaba, "sure that destiny will lead my feet aright."

"Thy faith is right," answered the old man,

"and I would not shake it for a moment. Still if knowledge may be gained, it would be well for you to seek it. And gained it may be. In Kaf the Simorg, the Bird of Ages, has his abode. There is nothing that he does not know. He has seen the children of men thrice destroyed. The .path is long and dangerous, but the Bird could direct your way to a certainty."

Thalaba gave ready heed to his word, and on the morrow pursued his journey.

CHAPTER X.

THE MAGIC THREAD.

THALABA travelled on day after day. He crossed rivers, and climbed mountains, and plodded wearily across measureless plains, but saw neither man, nor the trace of man. It was a cold country which he now reached, and such slender provision of food as he had carried was exhausted. The sun was not to be seen in the sky; but there was one dull cloud over all, and now the snow began to fall. How he wished for his native deserts and the warm winds of Arabia! And now the night came on, and there was neither moon nor star to be seen; only a dim light reflected from the snow. At last he spied a fire burning in a cave of the hill, and to that, with courage and strength renewed, he moved on.

He found a woman in the cave, a solitary

woman, who sat spinning by the fire and singing as she span. She had grey hair, but her face was smooth like a girl's. She smiled a welcome to him; but still went on with her spinning and singing. He laid his bow before the fire, for its string was frozen stiff, and his quiver also, for the feathers on the arrows were covered with ice. Then he asked for food. She answered him in song.

> "The She-bear, she dwells near to me,
> And she hath cubs, one, two, three;
> She hunts the deer, and brings him here,
> And then with her I make good cheer.
> And now to the chase the She-bear is gone,
> And she with her prey will be here anon."

When she had said this she began her spinning again. The thread gleamed like gold in the blaze of the pine-log, but it was so marvellously fine, that except when the light fell on it you might look for it in vain. Thalaba looked on with wonder, and she observing him, spoke again, this time also in song.

> "Now twine it round thy hands I say,
> Now wind it round thy hands I pray,
> But he must be
> O stronger than thee,
> Who can break this thread of mine!"

Thalaba, thinking no harm, so sweetly did she smile on him, took the thread, and wound it round and round his right hand, and round and round his left. Then the woman spoke again—

"Now thy strength, O stranger, strain,
Strain and break the slender chain."

Thalaba strained his strength, but to no purpose, till he was flushed with shame and fear. Then the witch, for the woman was the witch Maimuna, smiled at him again, but this time fiercely, and she sang a fourth time—

"I thank thee, I thank thee, Hodeirah's son,
For binding thyself in the chain I have spun."

With this she wrenched a lock of hair from his head, and sang again—

"Sister! Sister! hear my voice,
The thread is spun,
The prize is won,
The work is done,
For I have made captive Hodeirah's son."

And in a moment Khawla, the fiercest of the sorcerers, was there in her magic chariot. And when she saw the youth she laughed aloud in scorn, and clapped her hands for joy. That moment the She-bear came in from the chase, bearing the deer that it had caught in its mouth. This she laid down at Maimuna's feet, and looked up wistfully as if to ask for her share.

"There! there!" said Maimuna, and pointing to Thalaba, spurned him with her foot. "There! make thy meal of him."

And the two sisters laughed aloud, but the She-bear fawned upon the youth and licked his hand. Thereupon Maimuna stamped on the ground, and called a spirit up.

"Shall we bear the Enemy to the dungeon of the Domdaniel Cavern?"

"Woe to our Empire if he ever tread the Domdaniel Cavern."

"Shall we leave him fettered here to die of hunger now?"

"Fly from your dwelling, I see danger at hand, danger that he should live and thou shouldst fall."

"Whither then shall we carry him?"

"To Mohareb's Island."

So they threw Thalaba ·chained into the magic chariot. Drawn by no mortal steed, it passed over land and sea, till it came to the island and to the chief city in which Mohareb reigned.   The Sultan himself came out to meet them in his royal robes, and Thalaba knew him at once as the one whom he had cast down into the pit amidst the ruins of Babylon.

The two sisters and Mohareb held council.

"Go up, and read the stars," said Khawla.

Maimuna went up to the terrace of the topmost tower, and stood there, her white hair streaming like the Aurora in the polar sky. When she descended, they asked, "What have you read?"

"Death—danger—judgment," said she.

"Is that what the stars say?" cried Khawla; "they are the creatures of Him who made them, and would terrify us with their lying threats.   I never liked this lore of the Heavens. Better much the sacrifice of Divination, and I will be my own oracle.   Command the victims, Mohareb.   You know what are wanted, that they must be male and female."

While the Sultan went to fetch them, Khawla made the place ready for the dreadful rite. She faced about to each point of the compass, and at each she laid her hand on the wall, and smote the air, and smote the floor, and said, " To Eblis and his slaves I consecrate this place. Let no one enter but he and they."

And now all was prepared. Mohareb returned, and the circle was drawn, and the victims were slain, and Khawla stood, holding a human head by the hair in either hand.

" Go out, ye lights ! " she cried, and began the spell. She spread out her arms, and whirled round, calling, " Eblis, Eblis," without ceasing, till she reeled with dizziness. Her hair stood up, and gave out sparks of light, and her eyes gleamed like the moon through a mist. Then she spoke—

> " Ye may hope, and ye may fear,
> The danger of his stars is near.
> Sultan ! if he perish, woe !
> Fate hath written one death blow
> For Mohareb and the foe !
> Triumph ! Triumph ! only she
> That knit his bonds can set him free ! "

Then she fell senseless on the ground. Mohareb and Maimuna knelt beside her, and wetted the palms of her hands with water, and her nostrils with blood till she revived.

"What did I say?" she asked. When she heard the words, her face grew dark. All that she said was, "Well, let him rot in prison."

But Mohareb read her purpose better. Her lips lied, but her face told the truth. They were pledged to him by oath ; but his death would keep them safe ; and he knew they would not spare him. Nor did the ring protect him, for they could strike at his life through Thalaba. It was needful, then, that he must take counsel for himself. Accordingly he went to the dungeon where the prisoner lay. It was early dawn, and Thalaba was so busy with his prayers, that the grating of the hinges did not rouse him. Mohareb stood still, and enviously watched the peace which piety can give.

When the youth had ended his prayer, and looked to see who his visitor might be, the Sultan said—"Arab, unknowingly you more than paid me for my guiding through that dangerous cave. The Hand that caught the Ring received me, and carried me whither I wished. See, I am not ungrateful. Take again the amulet."

It was but a show of gratitude. In truth he

gave the Ring that Thalaba's life might be safe, and with Thalaba's, as Khawla's oracle had warned him, his own. The youth took the Ring, and put it on his finger with the same words that he had used at first. " In the name of God! If its power be for good, well; if for evil, then God and my faith in Him shall hallow it."

Mohareb said, " You are brave, and I would willingly be your friend, aye, and buy your friendship for a royal price. Now hear me— There are two Powers in the world, two hostile Gods, equal in all things. Nay, hear me patiently—I say, *equal.* Look about you. The same earth bears fruit and poison. The Elements now are the servants of Man, and now his masters. If there is joy in one house, there is sorrow in the next. You say that sin entered into the world, and that God permits it to remain for a time. Nay, but if a serpent creep into your tent you crush it. Be sure that God had crushed His enemy if He could. No, Thalaba ; good and evil are but words. In Heaven as in earth it is the weak who are guilty. Think not that the dead are sent to abodes of bliss and evil. Not so, they join the great armies that fight the great fight. Woe to the vanquished! You, Thalaba, have chosen your part ill. The Power you serve is a hard taskmaster, and where are His wages? Who has ever seen them? But look at ours, the power and riches and pleasures of the world. Do you remember how we met at Babylon, each zealous for His Lord, adventurers both of us? Now think what I am, and what you are—you a prisoner, I the Sultan of this land."

Thalaba answered, "And this is your faith! monstrous falsehood which even the sun and moon and stars in their courses disprove. No; the true Master of the world is the Power of Good, and He will triumph in the end. You have me here in chains, but I am not deserted. And against you are leagued the Just and Wise of all time; yes, and your own crimes, and truth, and God in Heaven."

"Slave!" cried Mohareb, in his rage. "Slave, I leave you here; and in this prison you shall rot limb from limb," and he rushed out of the prison.

Meanwhile Khawla the witch was working

her spells against the life of Thalaba. She made an image of wax, compounding it of the wax of the machineal tree and the poison of the mandrake. This image she moulded to the shape of Thalaba, and muttered spells over it, by which it became instinct with a portion of the young man's life. Then she built up a pile of poisonous woods, and set the image of wax in the full blaze of the heat. She might as well have tried the eternal ice which is piled about the pole. "Waste away!" she cried, "and with thee waste Hodeirah's son!" But the flames harmed it no more than the moonbeam thaws a field of snow. "Curse thee!" cried the witch, "hast thou still a spell of safety?" and she threw the image into the fire itself, and in the fire itself it lay unharmed. Then she stamped thrice on the floor of the cave crying "Maimuna," and in a moment her sister was there.

When Maimuna saw the fire and the image she said, "Nay, sister, Mohareb's life is bound up with Thalaba's, and to Mohareb we are pledged by oath."

"Fool!" answered Khawla, "one must die

or all. To keep faith with Mohareb were to commit treason against all the rest of our company. But tell me what it is that protects the son of Hodeirah?"

For still the wax lay unmelted. So hot was the fire that the bat clinging to the roof of the cave loosed its hold sickening to death with the heat, and the toad, having crawled to the darkest corner, panted with fever, while the viper came out with her brood, and sported with them in the rays. But the image lay cold as marble.

At length Maimuna raised her thoughtful eyes. "Where, sister, did you find the wax? Was it the work of the bee, or of the worm? If so, your labour is lost. It is only the wax from a dead man's grave that can avail."

"Excellent witch," said Khawla. "Go and fetch it, for you know the place and the way."

And Maimuna went to fetch it. By her spells she opened a grave. What she there saw were too horrible to tell. But the terror of it so wrought upon her that she cast herself upon the earth in the agony of despair. And she had died the utter death but that it was that mysterious night on which all created things adore their Maker ; yes, all things, beasts and birds and fishes of the sea, and even trees and stones, all things but man only. And now, by the mercy of God, all the gracious influences of the time were poured out upon her, till she wept ; and at the sight of her tears her good angel came down again and took again his charge.

Maimuna thought to herself, " I will undo as far as I may the evil that I have done," and in a moment she was in the prison cell of Thalaba. One more spell, and only one will she work. She sang as she had sung when she had bound the silken threads about the prisoner's hands, and when she had finished he was free. But the prison walls are thick. She calls the Genii, but they do not hear ; her power was gone ; then she cried, " Rebel Spirits, in the name of God, hear me !" and in a moment the prison walls were burst open, and the two, Maimuna and Thalaba, were carried forth in the chariot of the winds.

CHAPTER XI.

LEILA.

IN another moment the two found themselves
again in the cave among the hills ; and Maimuna
felt the burden of her years fall upon her, for
she had prolonged her life far beyond the span
appointed to men by the magic of her spells.
So she died in faith and peace, and Thalaba
buried her in the snow, and taking his bow and
arrows from the hearth, where they had lain
since the witches had carried him away bound,
went on his way.   The wind blew keenly from
the East, and drifted the snow in his face, and
froze the breath upon his lips, till he was
almost spent with cold and hunger.   At last
he saw a light in the darkness, and though he
feared another snare from the magic arts of his
enemies, he had no choice but to make for it.

It was a little cottage in the middle of a

garden ; and, strange to say, the air of the garden was as mild as a summer wind, for a fountain of fire sprang up in the centre of it, sending rivulets of warmth streaming over it every way. Thalaba saw a door open, and went in. A girl lay asleep upon a couch, but woke at the sound of his steps. She rose, and took his hand, with gladness dancing in her eyes. But when she felt it cold, the smile died from her face, and she said, " I thought it would be warm like mine, but you are like the rest."

Thalaba stood surprised and silent. At last he answered—" Cold ? Lady, what wonder ! I have been travelling in this icy wilderness till the life is nearly frozen in me."

" You are a man then ? "

" Surely ; I did not think that grief and labour could have so changed me."

" And you can be warm sometimes, life-warm as I am ? "

" Surely, Lady ; I am subject as other men to heat and cold. You see a traveller who is bound upon hard adventures, and asks shelter for the night, meaning to pursue his journey to-morrow."

" No ; not to-morrow. You must not go so soon. And whither ? All the country round is ice and snow and deserts of endless snow over which no man can pass."

" He that has led me so far will support me still through cold and hunger."

"Hunger !" said the girl, and clapped her hands.

In a moment the table was spread with food, but whence and how it came no one could see.

"Why do you look, Mortal ? " said the girl ; "I made it come."

" But whence ? "

"What matter ? My father sent it. But I see you are no man ; if you were, your hunger would not let you ask such questions."

" I will not eat. It is the work of magic. Deceit and danger surround me. I was a fool to think I could escape them."

" Begone, insolent creature ! Do you fancy that I am plotting harm against you ? One day you will be sorry for having so wronged me."

" Hear, Lady ; I have many enemies, and my

way is beset with dangers. Thus I have learnt
to be suspicious. But if I have wronged you,
pray pardon me. In the name of God, I will
eat of your food."

"Just now you were afraid of sorcery, and
yet you have said a charm."

"A charm?"

"Yes, or what meant your words? I have
heard many spells and many names that rule
the Genii and the Elements, but that which
you said I have never heard."

"What! never heard the name of God?"

"Never; but you are a strange man. Why
this wonder and trouble? You must not
suspect me twice. If you are afraid, depart."

"Do you not know the God who made
you?"

"Who made me? My father made me, and
this house, and garden, and the fountain of fire;
and he makes men and women out of the snow
every morning. They can move and talk, but
they are always cold as ice, and in the evening
they melt away into nothing and I am alone.
How glad I am when my dear father comes!
Were it not for him, I would gladly melt away
like them."

"And have you always lived here?"

"Ever since I can remember."

"And you do not know your father's art?"

' No; I asked him once to give me some share of his power, but he shook his head and said that it was too dearly bought."

"Why did he put you here in the wilderness?"

"For fear and love. He said that the stars threatened a danger to my life, and he put me here amidst everlasting snow where no foot could ever come. And if indeed the enemy should come, I have a Guardian."

"A Guardian?"

"Yes; would you see him?"

So the girl led Thalaba through the garden. As they went, she said, "I do not think you are the enemy. But if you have any evil thought in your heart, depart in peace. I will not lead you to your death."

"Let him kill me," cried the youth, "if I have a single thought of harming you!"

And now they came to the place where the Guardian stood. It was an image of iron, with every vein and limb and muscle true to life. The knee was bent forward; the other stood firm and upright. The right hand was lifted ready to throw the thunder-bolt. When Thalaba approached, the Image knew the Destroyer, and hurled the thunder-bolt. But again the Ring, which Mohareb had restored to him, saved him. So blindly do the wicked work the will of Heaven! The lightning was turned back harmless. He started and looked round on the girl. He leant pale and breathless against a tree; the next moment she started with a scream of joy, "Save me, save me, Okba; the Enemy is here!"

"Okba!" said the youth, for he had never forgotten the name of his father's murderer since the Spirit had told it to him at midnight in Moath's tent. "Okba!" and he seized an arrow in his hand, and rushed at him.

"Son of Hodeirah!" said the old man, "my hour is not yet come. But my Leila, my innocent daughter, you may slay; this vengeance God allows."

Leila stood with her hands clasped round her father's neck, her eyes wide open with terror.

"It is not upon her that the blood of Hodeirah cries for vengeance." And again he threatened the Sorcerer, and again he felt his hand held by some mysterious power.

"You do not aim the blow more eagerly," said Okba, "than I would rush to meet it. But that would be but a poor revenge. No, I must suffer in my innocent child. Strike her, why do you delay ? God permits, nay, commands, the deed."

"Liar !" cried Thalaba, and Leila looked up wondering in her father's face.

"Nay !" said he, "'tis the truth. Long ago I saw this danger. I saw it in the stars at her birth, and when I called up a Spirit, and asked him, he said, 'One must die, Leila or Thalaba.' Yes ; and I mounted to the seventh heaven, and read the death table in which are written all the names of them that are for death, and her name was among them. Be merciful, young man ; and do not keep her any longer in her agony."

Then the rush of wings was heard, and Azrael, the Angel of Death, stood before them.

"Son of Hodeirah," said he, "the Magician speaks truth. I am come to receive the maiden's life at your hands."

"Hear me, angel," said Thalaba. "I have dared every danger, I have lost all that my soul holds dear. I have cut off every tie of life to avenge my father's death, and to root out of the earth the accursed sorcerer here. And I am willing to endure whatever still remains. But this innocent girl I will not slay. No, angel, I dare not do it!"

"Remember," said the angel, "every word of thine is written down, and thou must be judged for all."

"Be it so. He that reads the secrets of the hearts will judge me; I will not harm the innocent."

Then a voice came out of the darkness. "Think again, son of Hodeirah! One must die, Leila or Thalaba. She dies for thee, or thou for her. Think again, and weigh it well."

He did not hesitate a moment; but reaching out his hand cried, "Oneiza, receive thy Thalaba unstained by crime."

"Thou hast disobeyed. The hour is mine,"

cried Okba, and shaking his daughter off, drew the dagger from his side, and aimed a deadly blow.

He aimed it, but Leila rushed between to save the youth, and sank into Thalaba's arms, and Azrael from his hands received her parting soul.

CHAPTER XII.

WHEN Okba saw that his daughter was dead, he threw himself on her dead body in a passion of grief, now crying out to the powers of Hell to help him, and then to Heaven to strike him dead, and then again cursing Thalaba. But the youth stood by in silent pity. As he stood, he felt his cheek suddenly fanned by a motion of the air, and looking round saw that it came from the wings of a green bird that was hovering near him. And now the bird perched on his hand, and turned a gentle eye to him, as if to win his confidence. Then it sprang up and flew forward, and then returned and perched as before, manifestly inviting him to follow. Thalaba obeyed the call, and under the moonlight pursued his way across the river. And now the morning sun came out, and the bird still flew before him; all the day long it was his guide, but when the evening came, leaving a purple light on the range of hills to which his steps were bent, it vanished out of his sight. For a while Thalaba thought that it had left him. But when he had made his evening prayer, and lifted his head from the ground, he saw a speck in the air; nearer it came, and nearer, till he saw that it was his guide. The bird hung hovering before the traveller, and in her foot she clasped a cluster of fruit that she had brought from the woods of Paradise. Thalaba took and ate, and felt all his powers renewed. In his fresh strength he climbed with untired feet the steep ascent of the hills, and the bird still guided him, till in the very heart of the mountains a valley opened before his eyes. It was the Simorg's Valley, the dwelling of the Bird of Ages.

On a green mossy bank beside a rivulet the Bird of Ages stood. Thalaba approached, and crossing his arms upon his breast, thus spoke: " Earliest and wisest of all things that are, guide me, I beseech thee, on my way. I am

The Simorg.

bound for the Caverns under the rocks of the ocean, where the Sorcerers have their dwellings. How may I reach them?"

The Simorg opened his eyes, and said, "Go northward by the stream. In the fountain of the Rock wash away thy stains. Then fortify thy soul with prayer. Thus prepared, climb on the sledge. Be bold ; be cautious. Seek and find, for God has appointed all."

Then he was silent, and returned to his repose.

Thalaba went northward along the rivulet's side, tracing it to its source, and the green bird went with him till they reached the Fountain of the Rock. There the youth washed away his stains, and fortified his soul with prayer, and the bird stood meanwhile near the youth, thinking of all the perils through which he must pass.

When he had finished ablution and prayer, he saw a sledge under a pine-tree, and the dogs harnessed to it, and the dogs were watching him with their ears erect and their eyes wide open. They were as lean as dogs could be, and black but for one white line like the new moon upon their breasts. Thalaba took his place in the sledge, and the bird perched on his knees, and when the dogs, turning their heads, saw that he was seated, they started. Up the icy path they hastened, and when they reached the top, they stood still and panted, and looked back to the youth, as if pleading for pity, and moaned and whined with fear.

And now they start again on the downward path. It was narrow and steep, with a wall of rock on one side, and a precipice on the other. One sway of the sledge will send the traveller headlong on to the rocks below. And still the dogs barked and whined, and though Thalaba sat with his arms folded, and had neither scourge nor goad, the blood flowed fast from their skin and tracked the way with red. And now on a height above the path a giant fiend stands ready to thrust down an avalanche. If Thalaba looks back, he dies. But he is brave, and the dogs are swift, and the thunder of the falling avalanche echoes far behind. So they reach the plain.

It was a desolate expanse with neither grass nor bush nor tree. The dogs went quickly on their way ; but when the sun went down, they stopped and looked at Thalaba. He knelt on the ground, and said his prayer, and they knelt beside him, the tears running down their cheeks. This done they lay close together, as close as they could lie, and slept : and Thalaba slept, lying backward in the sledge, and the green bird slept, nestling in his breast.

At dawn the dogs woke him, and knelt again with him while. he prayed. And all that day and many days afterwards they travelled across the plain, halting at the hour of prayer, and the bird was a companion to Thalaba by day, and rested in his breast at night.

And now the signs of life begin to appear. First is seen the fir, then the laurel with down-curving arms, then the quivering leaves of the aspen, then the poplar, and the light and peaceful birch. Now, too, Thalaba can see the track of the deer, and the ermine running over the snow, and hear the whirr of the grouse's wings among the pines ; now, too, the owl follows his sledge, and soon he hears the song of the thrush, till at last he comes to bushes and grass, and thickets bright with red berries, and to flowers.

Now was the last morning of their journey, and the green bird fixed on Thalaba an entreating eye. At that moment speech was given her.

"Servant of God," she said, "if I have guided you right, give me what I ask."

"Ask what you will, I shall still be your debtor."

"Son of Hodeirah, when you shall see an old man bent under the burden of his punishment, forgive him, yea, and pray for him."

Thalaba's cheek flushed, and he looked to the bird as if half repenting his promise, for he thought of Okba, and remembered his father's dying groan.

The bird saw his doubt, and spoke again. "O Thalaba, if she who received the blow of the dagger to save you deserves one kind remembrance, save the father whom she loves from endless death."

"What, Leila, is it you? What is it I dare refuse to you? This is no time to harbour thoughts of revenge in my heart. Here I put them off for ever. God pardon me as I pardon him. But who am I that I should save a sinful soul?"

"Enough! When the hour is come, remember me!" And she spread her wings and soared to Paradise.

And now the dogs start forward on their journey. It was still early morning when they reached the well-head of a rock. The little pool was clear and deep. It was stirred strangely below, but its surface was calm; and on it there lay a little boat. It had neither oar nor sail, only a rudder, and by the rudder stood a Damsel.

The dogs looked wistfully at her, and their tongues were loosed. "Have we done well, dear Mistress?" they asked.

The Damsel answered—"Poor servants of God, when all this witchery is destroyed, your woes and mine will end. This new adventurer gives us a new hope. God forbid that he like you should perish for his fears! But now sleep, and wait the end in peace."

As she spoke a deep sleep fell upon them. Then the Damsel said to Thalaba, "Will you come with me? The way is strange and dangerous; but the wretched ask your help. Will you come?"

"I will come in the name of God," said Thalaba, and stepped into the boat.

The stream ran on through pleasant fields, with flowers blooming at the side, and willows dipping their boughs into its waters, and the dragon-flies, bright with green and gold, skimming over its surface. And now it was swollen by many a rivulet and rill, and grew into a great river, with banks that widened as they went.

"Will you come with me?" asked the Damsel again.

"Go on, in the name of God," answered Thalaba.

And now they are come to the sea; and the Damsel asked him a third time, "Will you come?" and Thalaba answered as before.

And now they see the land, and the caverns frowning on the rocks. The Damsel said— "See that cavern, our path is under its arch. But now it is the ebb, and before the flood we cannot pass over the rocks. Go and perform your last ablutions on the rocks and strengthen your heart with prayer. I too have need of prayer."

And she guided the boat with a firm hand through the breakers, and Thalaba leapt out upon the shore.

CHAPTER XIII.

THE DOOM.

THALABA drew Abdaldar's Ring from his finger, and threw it into the sea. "I will trust in nothing but in Thee, O God," he cried. This done he lay down on the beach to rest, for his heart was not yet calm enough for prayer. And now he felt that there was some spiritual presence near him.

Then there came a voice, " Thalaba," and the youth knew the voice of Moath ; and after this a second and a dearer voice that said, " Thalaba, go on, and finish your work. Let me no longer suffer hope."

Thalaba looked eagerly to the sea, and as he looked the Damsel drove the little boat to the land, saying, "Come."

He leapt on board.

" Have you had comfort in your prayer?" she asked.

" Yes," said he, " a heavenly visitation."

" God be praised," she answered, " then I have not hoped in vain," and her voice trembled, and the tears ran down her cheeks. She went on : " Stranger, in years long past there was one who vowed himself as you have done, the Champion of the Lord against the Sorcerer race. He was young and gentle and brave, a lion-hearted man. He loved me, and I kept him from his calling, till the hour was past, and the angel who should have crowned him smote him in anger. Years and years have passed, and in his place of penance he waits for the Deliverer. Surely you are he !"

As she spoke, they came to the entrance of the cave, and passed beneath the arch. The sea-birds were screaming from their nests, and yet not in fear, for they did not know the shape of man. As they went on, the light grew dimmer and more dim till they came to where the waters lapped on the rock that bounded them. There two doors of adamant closed up the passage. On the rock beside sat a hoary-headed man, watching an hour-glass.

"Is it the hour appointed?" asked the Damsel.

The old man neither answered her nor lifted his eyes, but the sands were now running low in the glass. When the last were gone, he lifted up his hand and struck the gates. The gates opened at the stroke, and the Damsel said, "Go on; I wait you here."

Not for a moment did he tarry, not one look did he cast behind him, but hastened on. There was a yellow light in the cavern such as may be seen upon the hills at sunset when the sun shines through the mist upon the hills; the path still was downward till it ended in a precipice. Black as night was the abyss, and over the depth was a little car supported by four wings, living wings, but without body or head and unfeathered, springing from one stem. And on the brink, fastened with fiery fetters to the rocks, lay a young man. It was he who had lingered over the appointed hour, neglectful in the arms of love.

Thalaba exclaimed, "Servant of God, can I help you?"

"I have sinned," said he, "and I endure my

punishment with patience. The hour that sees the destruction of the Sorcerer race will set me free."

"Is it not come? Verily it has by this token," and with fearless hand he grasped the burning fetters, tore them from the rock, and threw them blazing into the pit. Then for a moment the vapours kindled by the fire flamed up, then all was dark again.

" Deliverer!" cried the youth, "and where is she?"

" Lo! she waits for you at the gates."

" And you will join us in your triumph?"

"Wait not for me; my path has been appointed."

" But your name? that we may spread it abroad in the world and bless thee."

" Bless the Merciful;" so saying, Thalaba murmured the name of God, and leapt into the car. Down it sailed a measureless depth, till at last it struck upon the rock.

Thalaba stood dazed and giddy for a time with the shock; then looking round he saw a distant light, small as a speck, but most intense. Beyond all was darkness. " It is no friend," thought he to himself, " that the darkness hides." And indeed it was true. For a rebel Afreet, largest of his kind, lay on the ground at the gate of the Sorcerers' cave. He scented the approach of human food, and the lust of hunger burned fiercely in his eye. Thalaba went on, shading his eyes with his hand, and when he came within due distance laid an arrow in the rest, and fixing his gaze resolutely on the light, loosed the bow. It pierced the Afreet where he lay ; and he sent up a cry so hideous and so loud that no human voice could equal it.

Thalaba stepped across the monster as he lay in the agonies of death, and smote on the doors of stone, bidding them in the name of God give way. The rocks shuddered at the sound, and the doors were rent asunder, and in a moment he saw the Teraph, and the Fire, and Khawla, and Mohareb armed, ready for conflict. Thalaba struck his raised arm with numbing force, and rushed by, for he saw amongst the flames Hodeirah's holy sword. Then Khawla met the youth, and leapt upon him, and clasped him with close clinging arms, while she bade Mohareb smite the deadly blow. He spurned

her to the ground, and when she rose again and clung about his knees, he seized her leathery neck with a throttling grasp, and thrust her aside, and sprang forward to the sword. The flames knew the Destroyer, and curled around him, and coiled up his robe, and made a crown on his head.

The moment that Thalaba had laid his hand upon his father's sword the Living Image in the inner cave smote the round altar. Then all the Domdaniel Cavern rocked to its foundations, and the earth felt the shock. All the Sorcerer race, wherever dispersed, felt and obeyed the summons; such was the compulsion laid upon them by the Covenant of Hell. They were sworn to meet the common danger and to share the common doom. And now they crowded round the Destroyer, vainly endeavouring to crush the single foe. First of all was Mohareb, for the witch had foretold that one blow would be fatal to Thalaba and to him; and now, despairing of his own safety, he sought to uphold the cause of Eblis.

But none can withstand the Destroyer armed as he is with the fated sword. Mohareb lifts his shield to parry the stroke, and it is shorn in two. He lifts his scymetar, and the broken hilt hangs from his hand, and now he bleeds, he flies, he strives to hide himself in the crowd. They too feel the sword; they fly to the inner cave, and fall fearfully about the Giant Idol's feet.

It was a Living Image made by magic art of flesh and bone and human blood. It had the shape of Eblis, in strength and stature such as he was of old when he stood among the Sons of God pre-eminent, Lucifer, Son of the Morning. In one hand he grasped a sceptre, with which he had power to shake the earth, and raise the sea in storms, and lay cities in ruins, with the other he sustained the weight of the sea, for the cavern was roofed with the waters.

Now the Sorcerers lay trembling round his feet; and Mohareb clung about his knees. The Idol was pale and calm with excess of fear, for he knew the Destroyer. Sure of his stroke and without haste Thalaba advanced. Okba met him on his way, the only fearless man of all that miserable company.

"Strike me," he cried, " I am he that stole at midnight into thy father's tent. This is the hand that pierced Hodeirah's heart. This is the hand that was red with the blood of thy brothers and sisters. Let the vengeance fall on me," and he spread his bosom to the stroke.

"Old man," said Thalaba, " I strike thee not. The harm that thou hast done to me and mine has brought its own bitter punishment. I pardon thee for thy daughter's sake. For her sake repent while it is yet time."

Okba stood astonished, and his heart was softened, and his tears gushed out. Then was heard a voice.

"Thou hast done well, my Servant. Ask and receive thy reward."

Thalaba said, " I have but wished to do my duty. But look on this Sorcerer, many are his crimes, but mercy is infinite. If I have found favour, let his soul be saved from utter death."

The Voice replied, " The prayers of penitence never arise unheard. Ask for thyself."

"I am alone on earth," said Thalaba, " do with me as thou wilt."

Then came no answering voice. But the

spirit of Hodeirah came to see the work of vengeance accomplished, and by the side of Hodeirah, a pure form clothed with rosy light, was Zeinab. Then Thalaba knew that his hour was come. He leapt forward and plunged his sword hilt-deep into the Idol's heart. The domed vault fell in, and all the tribe of the Sorcerers perished together, but Oneiza received her husband into the bowers of Paradise.

THE STORY OF RUSTEM.

THE STORY OF RUSTEM.

CHAPTER I.

OF ZAL, THE FATHER OF RUSTEM.

A CERTAIN great Persian hero, San by name, after being childless for many years, had a son born to him. The child was as fair as the sun, but, by a strange misfortune, his hair was white. For seven days no one dared to tell the father what had happened—that his beautiful wife had brought into the world an infant like an old man. At last the child's nurse, who was as bold as a lioness, went bravely to him, and said, " Sire, I bring you good news. May your days be happy! May the heart of your enemies be torn asunder! God has granted you the desire of your heart. You have a son, who, small as he is, yet shows the heart of a lion. A beautiful child he is, and you will see nothing amiss in him, except that by some ill-luck his hair is white. Fate would have it so. Be content, my lord, with what God has given you."

On this the hero came down from his throne, and went to the apartments of the women. There he saw a child, of a singular beauty, but with the head of an old man, such as he had never seen or even heard tell of before. The sight struck him with despair. He lifted his eyes to heaven, and said, " O God, all that Thou ordainest is for good. If I have done any evil, if I have departed from the faith, accept my repentance, and pardon my sin. Truly my soul is overwhelmed with shame that I have had a son born to me who seems to be of the race of Satan, with his black eyes and his hair white as a lily. What shall I say when the nobles come to me? What shall I say about this child of a demon? Verily I shall be compelled to leave Persia for very shame."

Thus cursing his lot, he ordered them to take the child and carry it to a mountain which they call Alburz, or the White Mountain, a lonely place which was never trodden by the foot of man. But, though his father cast off the innocent child, God did not forget him. A great bird, the Simorg by name, had its nest on the mountain, and, going out to look for food for its young, saw the child lying on the ground ; the thorns were his cradle, the hard earth his nurse. A day and a night he had lain there crying for hunger. God touched the heart of the Simorg with pity, so that it did not think of devouring the child, but, catching him up in its claws, carried him to its nest upon the mountain. The young of the great bird were not less kind to him ; indeed they showed him a marvellous pity, so astonished were they at his beauty. As for the Simorg, it chose out for its guest the tenderest part of its prey ; and the poor child, for want of milk, was nourished on blood. Thus he grew up, sometimes remaining in the nest, and sometimes wandering in the forests on the mountain side. He was straight and tall as a cypress-tree, and the report of his beauty and strength was carried far and wide.

After a while San had a dream. He thought

that he saw a rider mounted on an Arab steed, and that this rider came to him and gave him news of his son. When he woke, he called his nobles to him, and told them his dream.

"Do you think it possible," said he, "that the child survives the cold of winter and the heat of summer?"

Old and young answered him with one voice —"You were ungrateful to God for His gift. The sight of the child's white hair threw you into despair, but what was that in a body so fair? And now prepare to look for him. Do not fancy that he is dead. He whom God regards with favour will not perish either of cold or heat."

So San went to Mount Alburz with a great company of followers to look for his son. When he came to the mountain side he saw a great rock which seemed to pierce the very skies, so high was it. On this was a great nest, built of trunks of ebony and sandal-wood, interlaced with branches of aloes. Walking round the edge of this nest was a young man of tall stature, and San saw that the young man was like himself; but he could find no way up to the nest. Then, bowing his head to the ground, he cried, " I implore forgiveness for my sins. If this child be not the child of a demon, but of my own race, be merciful to me, and help me to climb to this nest." God heard his prayer and granted it.

When the Simorg saw San and his followers he said to Zal, " I have been as a mother to you ; but now your father, the hero San, has come for you, and I must give you up to him safe and sound."

The young man was sorry to hear this, and said (he had never seen the face of man, but the Simorg had taught him to speak) : " Are you tired of my company ? Your nest is as good as a throne to me."

The Simorg said, " When you have seen a real throne, it may be that my nest will no longer seem all that you can desire. It is not for want of love that I send you away ; indeed I could have wished for nothing better than that you should have remained here ; but your lot in life is otherwise ordered. Take one of my feathers with you, and if ever you find yourself in a strait, throw it into the fire, and I

will come to your help. And do not forget
me, for the love that I have for you breaks my
very heart."

Thus speaking he took him up, and carried
him to his father. When San saw his son, he
perceived that he was worthy of a throne. He
was as strong as a lion; his eyelashes were
black, his eyes dark brown, his lips like coral,
his cheeks red as blood. The one fault in him
was his hair. San blessed his son, and clothed
him as became his birth, and gave him a
war-horse to ride, and called his name Zal.

Then the father and the son journeyed
together to pay their court to the great King
Minuchehr, and told him the story. The
King consulted the wise men, who told him
that Zal would become a great hero, both
prudent and brave. These prophecies so
delighted him that he gave San the richest
presents that can be imagined—Arab horses
with trappings of gold, Indian swords in gold
scabbards, rubies, pages clothed in brocades of
gold, embroidered with jewels, and, among
other splendid gifts, a throne adorned with
turquoises, and finally a charter that invested

him with the dominion of India and the East.

After this San made an expedition against the Kingdom of Mazenderan, the country of the Demons, leaving his kingdom in the charge of Zal, and Zal, having learnt all that he could from the wise men of the land, resolved to visit various parts of his dominions. Accordingly, he came to Cabul, which was a province tributary to his father, and was received with great honour by Mihrab, prince of that country. Mihrab would gladly have entertained him, but Zal said, "It is impossible; what would my people say if they heard that I drank wine and was the guest of an idolater? Ask me anything else, and you shall have it."

Now Zal's companions had described to him Rudabeh, the daughter of Mihrab, as being the very greatest beauty in the world; and it so happened that Mihrab himself said in his daughter's presence that there was no hero under the sun that could be compared to Zal. Thus the two came to love each other; and their love so increased, that it passed all limits of reason. But there was this hindrance to their marriage, that the lady came of an evil stock, the race of King Zohak, the cruellest tyrant that ever had lived upon the earth.

Zal put the matter before his father, and his father again asked the advice of his wise men. The wise men consulted the stars, and gave him this answer: "Great King, we have good news for you. The marriage of Zal and the daughter of Mihrab will be fortunate above all others. They shall have a son who shall be unmatched for strength and valour, who shall root out the wicked from the earth. He shall subdue the Tartars, and raise the kingdom of the Persians to the heavens."

When he heard this, he sent back the messenger whom Zal had sent to him with this answer: "This is a foolish passion of thine, my son; nevertheless, I will not hinder. Only we must see what King Minuchehr will say."

King Minuchehr assembled his wise men, and said to them, "My fathers broke down the power of the tyrant Zohak; and we must not let the foolish passion of Zal raise it up again. Mix these races together, and it will be like mixing a poison with some precious drug; and, indeed, if the child of these two should be like his mother rather than his father, there will be great troubles for Persia. Tell me what I should do."

But the wise men had no answer to give. Then the King sent for Prince San, who was now returning victorious from his expedition. The Prince came and related to him his adventures; but when he would have gone on to speak of his son and the Princess Rudabeh, the King interrupted him.

" Go," he cried, " and burn with fire the city of Mihrab. And as for Mihrab, and his family, let not one of them live. His nobles, his servants—kill them all."

He spoke with such fury that San dared not answer a single word. He bowed his head to the ground and departed, setting out that very day with his army for the land of Cabul.

Zal heard that he was coming, and went to meet him. When he came into his father's presence, he kissed the ground at his feet, and said, " Sire, your justice and goodness make all men happy except your son. When I was a new-born child, you left me to die upon the mountains; and now—what are you intending to do? I went to dwell in Cabul by your orders; it was for your pleasure that I performed the journey hither. And now you have brought an army to lay waste the country which I inhabit, and to slay the Prince who has welcomed me. This is the justice that you do to your son. See, I am in your hands; do with me as you will; cut me in pieces if it is your pleasure. But know that all the harm you do to Cabul, you do to me."

San answered: "You are right; you say nothing but what is just and right. But wait and see whether I cannot help you. I will write a letter to the King, and you shall carry it to him yourself."

San wrote a letter in which he pleaded the cause of his son. " I behaved very ill to him once," he said, "and I promised that I would never again refuse him a request; and now he has set his heart on marriage. For myself I have asked neither provinces nor honours; and for him, great King, I ask only that you should deal with him after your wisdom."

Zal carried the letter to the King, who received him with all honour and kindness. "You have brought up again," he said, "an old sorrow; your father's letter troubles me; but he and you shall have your desire. Wait a while till I can consult my wise men."

The wise men spent three whole days and nights in searching into the secrets of the heavens. Then they came to the King and said, "We have inquired into the movements of the stars, and they tell us this—the child that shall be born to the son of San and the daughter of Mihrab shall be a great hero. He shall have long life, courage, strength, and glory. No man shall be his match in the battle or at the banquet. He shall catch lions in his hunting nets, and roast a wild ass whole for his meal."

The King said, " Keep secret what you have told me. I will put the young man's wit to the proof. Ask him questions that shall try him."

The first sage said to him : " I saw twelve trees, fair and tall. Each puts forth thirty branches ; and they neither increase nor diminish."

The second said : " I saw two noble horses, one black as a sea of pitch, the other bright as crystal. They are always running at full speed, and cannot gain one on the other."

The third said : " I saw thirty knights passing before the King ; I counted them and I found one wanting ; I counted them again, and there were thirty."

The fourth said : " I saw a garden filled with green things, and abounding with water. A strong man came into it, carrying a sharp scythe. He cut down the green and the dry alike. If you cried to him for pity he would not listen."

Zal reflected a while on these questions, and then answered : " The twelve fair trees that have each thirty branches and neither increase nor diminish are the twelve months, each of which has thirty days, neither more nor less. —The two noble horses, of which one is black, the other white, that are always pursuing each other, are night and day. They fly like a wild beast before a dog, and neither gains upon the other.—As for the thirty knights, whose number seems to want one, but is complete if you count it again, it is in this : in every month there is one moon that is hidden from our eyes, but when you look again it is there.—And the man with the scythe, who cuts down the green and the dry alike, who listens to no complainings, he is time, and we are the grass which he cuts."

The King and all his nobles greatly applauded the wisdom of Zal. Then the King would try his strength. He bade some of his greatest warriors arm themselves, and Zal, on the other hand, armed himself. Zal looked among his adversaries for him who was the most famous and skilful of them all ; he burst out of the cloud of dust in which he was hidden like a leopard, seized his opponent by the girdle, and lifted him out of his saddle so lightly that the King and all his people were astonished. They cried with one voice, "There was never the equal of Zal!" and the King said, " Happy the father of such a son ! Unhappy the mother of him who shall meet him in battle !"

So Zal, having proved his wisdom and his courage to the satisfaction of the King, had his will, and married the daughter of Mihrab. In due time his wife bare him a son ; but before the birth she was so near to death that Zal was in despair. In the midst of his grief he bethought him of the feather which the Simorg had given him. This he took, and put it on the coals of a brazier ; before it was consumed the Simorg appeared.

"Do not vex yourself," said the wise Bird ; "so mighty a child cannot come into the world without great trouble. Give the mother this nut which I have brought with me, having first pounded it in milk and musk. And give her also strong drink that she may forget her pains."

Zal did as the Simorg told him ; after this all went well with the mother. When she awoke they brought her the child. He was but a day old, and yet he seemed to have been born a whole year ; and he was as fair as a nosegay of lilies and tulips. When his mother saw him, she smiled upon him, and said, "He shall be called Rustem." Now Rustem means deliverance.

CHAPTER II.

THERE was never in the world such a child as
Rustem, the son of Zal.   He was fed with the
milk of ten nurses, and when he was weaned,
his food was bread and meat, and he ate as
much as five men.   As for his strength and
stature, they were such as never had been seen
before or will be seen again.

One day he was sleeping in his chamber
when he heard outside his door a great cry that
the King's white elephant had broken its chain
and was at liberty, and that the inhabitants of
the palace were in great danger.   In a moment
he rushed to seize his grandfather's club, and
prepared to go out.   The attendants tried to
stop him.   "We dare not incur your father's
rage," they said, "by opening the door.   The

night is dark ; the elephant has broken his chain ; and yet you are going out. What folly is this!" Rustem was greatly enraged to be so hindered, and struck the man who spoke so terrible a blow between the head and the nape of the neck, that his head fell off like a ball with which children play. When he turned to the others they soon made way for him. Then he struck the door with his club, and burst the bolts and bars with a single blow. This done, he laid the club upon his shoulder, and hastened after the elephant. As for his warriors, they were all as frightened of the beast as a lamb is frightened of a wolf. When the furious beast saw him, it rushed at him, lifting its trunk to strike him. Rustem gave it one blow, for only one was wanted ; its legs failed under it and it fell ; you had said, so vast was it, that a mountain had fallen. Rustem returned to his chamber and finished his sleep.

The next day Zal, hearing what his son had done, sent for him, and covered him with praises. " My son," he said, " you are yet but a child, and yet there is no one to match you in courage and stature. I have an enterprise for you to conduct. Many years ago my grand-father was sent by the King to take an enchanted fortress which is situated upon Mount Sipend, and was killed by a rock that was thrown upon his head by one of the besieged, after he had attacked it in vain for a whole year. After this my father San assembled an army, and marched against the place. But he could never find the way which led to the place. It is indeed so well provided that no one need ever leave it to get anything from without. San indeed wandered for years over the deserts, looking for the fortress, but was obliged at last to return without having avenged his father's death. Now, my son, it is your turn. Go in disguise ; the keepers of the fort will not know you ; and when you have made your way into the fortress, destroy the wretches root and branch."

" I will do it," said Rustem.

Zal went on : " Disguise yourself as a camel-driver. Pretend that you are coming in from the desert, and that you have a cargo of salt with you. There is nothing in that country that they value more than salt. Let them once hear that this is what you are bringing, and great and small will welcome you."

Rustem gladly undertook this business. He hid the great club with which he had slain the white elephant in a load of salt, and he chose a number of companions who were as prudent as they were brave. Their arms also were hidden in loads of salt, and so they approached the fortress.

The keeper of the gate saw them from a distance, and ran to the Prince, saying, "A caravan with a number of camel-drivers has arrived. If you ask me for what purpose they have come, I should say that, in my opinion, they have salt to sell."

Accordingly the Prince sent a messenger to the master of the caravan, to ask him what his packages contained.

Rustem said, "Go back, and tell your master that I have salt in my packages."

The Prince, on receiving this message, in great joy ordered the gate to be thrown open, and Rustem with his camels and their drivers, and the packages which they had with them, all entered the fortress. Rustem was courteously greeted by the Prince, and greeted him courteously in return. Then he made his way to the Bazaar, taking his camel-drivers with him. The people crowded round him, some with clothing, others with gold and silver; all were eager for his merchandise; and there was not a thought of fear or suspicion in the heart of any one of them. When the night came on Rustem executed his plan of attack. First, he fell upon the Prince and levelled him to the ground with a single blow of his club. There was not a chief in the whole fortress that could stand before him. Some he struck down with his club, and some with his sword. When the morning came there was not a single man of all the defenders of the fortress that was not either dead or disabled.

In the middle of the fortress there was a building of stone with a gate of iron. Rustem gave a blow of his club to the gate, and it flew open before him. Within there was a great vaulted hall, full of gold pieces and pearls. There never was such a sight in the world.

Rustem sent a message to his father, to tell him of his victory, and to ask him what he should do.

Zal wrote back to this effect: " I send you herewith two thousand camels to carry away your booty. Load them with all that is precious, and then burn the place with fire."

This Rustem did. He loaded the camels with precious stones, and gold, and costly swords, chains and girdles, pearls and jewels worthy of a king, and Chinese brocades richly embroidered with figures. This done, he set fire to the fortress, and so departed.

All this Rustem did while he was yet a child.

CHAPTER III.

WHILE Rustem was growing to manhood, Persia suffered great troubles. First the good King Minuchehr died, and his successor, his son Newder, exercised his power very ill. When the news of this change came to the King of the Tartars, he conceived the idea of conquering the country for himself and avenging the Tartars, for all that they had ever suffered at the hands of the Persians. Accordingly he sent for his son Afrasiab, who was next to himself in the kingdom, and asked his advice. Afrasiab gave his voice for war, and though his younger brother counselled peace, he prevailed. So when the plains were covered with the green freshness of spring, the army of the Tartars set forth.

It was an unlucky hour for Persia, for the great hero San was just dead, and Zal, the white-haired, his son, was busy with his burial, and Rustem was sick. Nevertheless, King Newder raised as great an army as he could, and came to meet the invaders. On the first day of the battle, a Tartar champion, Barman by name, rode forth and challenged all the Persians to single combat. There was no one to answer except Kobad, who was the oldest warrior in the army. The old Kobad was killed, and afterwards the two armies fought together till the darkness separated them.

That night the two armies rested on the field of battle, and the next morning they renewed the conflict. A terrible struggle it was, and nothing in it was more dreadful than when King Newder himself charged out of his army to meet Afrasiab. They threw javelins at each other; they met with their lances; they even closed with each other like two serpents. At last, as night was coming on, Afrasiab began to prevail, and the king could scarcely escape. That day the Persians suffered far more loss than did their enemies; and when the darkness put an end for a while to the battle, they were greatly discouraged.

The king sent for two of his sons, and said to them—"My sons, the evil which my father prophesied has come upon us. He said : 'An army of Tartars will invade Persia, and you will be defeated.' Go to Mount Alburz, and there gather such as are still faithful to our house ; but go in secret, lest the army be discouraged. I know not whether I shall see you again ; I shall try my fortune once more. Be brave, be prudent ; and if ye hear bad news of me, know that it has been the will of heaven to afflict me." So saying, he embraced his sons and sent them away.

For two days the armies rested. Early in the morning of the third the battle began again. From morning till evening it raged so fiercely that the ground could not be seen for the dead. In the end the Persians suffered a great defeat ; and indeed, before many days were past, King Newder himself fell into the hands of Afrasiab, who slew him in a fit of rage on hearing that some of his bravest warriors had been killed by the Persians.

Some time after these things had happened, certain Persian nobles came to Zal and said—"The people are without a king; the Tartars oppress us, and you do not help us out of our troubles."

Zal said: "All my days I have feared nothing but old age; now it has come upon me, my back is bowed; I cannot wield the sword. But, thanks to God, the stump has put forth a noble shoot. My son Rustem will do all that you desire. But first I must find him a war-horse; the Arab horses are not strong enough for him."

Zal then called Rustem to him, and said: " My son, you are not yet come to the age of a soldier "—for he was yet but a boy—" can you meet the Tartar nobles on the field of battle? What say you ? "

"My father," said Rustem, "have you forgotten how I took the fortress of Mount Sipend, and killed the white elephant ? It would be a great disgrace if I were to be afraid of Afrasiab and his Tartars."

Still Zal was in doubt. " I remember, my son, what you have done; and yet I cannot help trembling. At your years you should be delighting yourself with music and song; you are not yet ready for battle."

Rustem answered—" I am not one to find any pleasure in peace. Give me the field of battle, and you shall see what I can do. But I must have a horse as strong as a mountain, which none but I shall be able to bridle ; and I must have a club such as none but I shall be able to wield."

Zal was delighted with this answer, and sent immediately to Zabulistan and Cabul for all the finest horses that could be found in them. They were all made to pass before Rustem, to whom the attendants explained the royal marks which were upon them. But every horse that Rustem took hold of, and put his hand upon its back, bent under the weight of his arm, till its belly touched the ground. At last came a . herd of horses from Cabul, and in it was a grey mare. She was as strong as a lioness ; but her height was but small. She was followed by a foal larger than herself.   Its eyes were black and bright—one could have seen them a mile away at night—its tail was arched, its hoofs were like steel. Its colour was saffron, with red spots. It was as strong as an elephant, as tall as a camel, and as vigorous as a lion. As soon as Rustem saw the colt, he made a knot in his lasso, and prepared to separate it from the rest of the herd. The keeper said to him—

" Noble sir, do not take that animal ; that belongs to another."

Rustem said, " To whom, then, does this horse belong ? I see no mark on his quarter."

" There is no need to look for a mark," said the old herdsman ; " the horse is famous enough. He is as light as water, and as swift as fire. We call him 'Raksh'—'Rustem's Raksh,' but we do not know who is his master. It is three years since he has been able to bear a saddle, and many nobles have desired to have him. But as soon as his mother sees a man's lasso, she runs up like a lioness to fight him. We do not know what secret is hidden under all this ; but take care, young man, to have nothing to do with this savage beast ; she will tear the heart out of a lion, and the skin off a leopard's back."

No sooner had Rustem heard this, than he

threw his lasso, and caught the spotted colt. The mare ran at him like a wild elephant, and would have seized his head in her teeth; but Rustem roared at her with so terrible a voice, that she stood still in astonishment. And as she stood, he dealt her a great blow on the head with his fist, so that she rolled in the dust. When she got up again, she sprang away and hid herself in the herd. Rustem tightened the knot of the lasso, and then pressed one of his hands with all his might on the colt's back. Raksh did not bend under it; one would have said, indeed, that he did not feel it. Rustem said to himself—

"That is my place; there I shall do great things."

He jumped on the colt's back, and said to the herdsman—

"Tell me what is the price of this horse."

"If you are Rustem," answered the herdsman, "mount him, and redress the wrongs of your country. His price is the land of Persia."

It was thus that Rustem got his great horse Raksh; never was there one that was swifter, or more sagacious, or more tractable.

CHAPTER IV.

RUSTEM FIGHTS WITH AFRASIAB.

ZAL marched with his army against the Tartars, Rustem leading the way. When he was within a few miles of the enemy, he assembled the veteran chiefs, and said—

"We have a great army; we have brave soldiers and wise counsellors; but we want union because we have no king. There is such a one as we want, the wise men tell me, at Mount Alburz; he is tall and strong, a lover of justice and truth, and he is of the royal race."

All the chiefs approved. Then Zal said to Rustem—

"Go at once to Mount Alburz; do homage to Prince Keïkobad, but do not stay with him; you must be back in fourteen days—and tell him that the army is asking for its king."

Rustem, in great joy, leapt upon the back of Raksh, and rode off at full speed. A number of Tartars had posted themselves upon the road, and attacked him. Club in hand, he fell upon them, and struck many to the ground, and drove the rest before him, so that they returned to Afrasiab full of terror.

Rustem meanwhile went on his way. When he was now about a mile from Mount Alburz, he saw a splendid palace standing in a beautiful garden. Near a fountain was placed a throne, on which sat a young man of singular beauty, with a circle of nobles round him. They invited Rustem to alight from his horse, and drink a cup of wine with them.

Rustem thanked them courteously, but said—

" I am bound for Mount Alburz on an errand of great importance, nor must I delay for an hour. All the borders of Persia are overrun with enemies ; in every house there is mourning, for the throne is without a king."

" If you are on your way to Mount Alburz," they said to him, " tell us who it is whom you want, and we will take you to him."

" There is there a king of the pure royal

race," answered Rustem; "his name is Keïko-bad. Tell me, if any one of you know, where I can find him."

" I know him," cried one of the young men; "come in, and I will tell you his character."

When Rustem learnt that he was to hear tidings about Keïkobad, he leapt from his horse, and went to where the nobles were sitting under the shade of the trees by the fountain.

The young man who had spoken to him seated himself on a chair, and holding Rustem's hand in one of his hands, filled with the other a cup of wine. He drank it to his guests, and gave another cup to Rustem.

"You ask me," he said, "about Keïkobad. How do you know his name?"

"Prince," said he, " I bring good tidings. The nobles of Persia have chosen Keïkobad to be their king; and my father, Zal, who is the chief among them, said to me—' Ride to Mount Alburz, find Keïkobad, and pay him homage on our behalf.' Tell me, then, where I can find him."

The young man smiled and said, " I am Keïkobad."

Rustem bowed his head, and coming down from his seat did homage to the King. The King called for a cup of wine, and touched it with his lips in Rustem's honour—and Rustem drained a cup in honour of the King.

The King said—" See, my dream has come true ; last night I dreamed that two falcons came to me by way of Persia, carrying a shining crown, and put it on my head. This is the reason why I assembled these nobles to meet you to-day."

The very same hour the two set out for Persia with a troop of horsemen. But when they came near the advanced posts of the Tartars, Kaloun, the great Tartar chief, came out to attack them.

When the King saw him and his followers, he was for giving him battle. But Rustem said—

" My lord, it does not become your greatness to fight in such a battle. My horse and my club, with God to help me, will be enough to deal with these enemies."

So saying he gave the rein to Raksh, and charged the Tartars. He caught one trooper from his horse, and striking another with the man as if he were a club dashed out his brains. He tore the riders out of their saddles, one after another, and dashed them upon the ground with such force as to break their skulls and necks and backs. Kaloun thought that it was a demon who had broken his chains, and was riding about with a club in his hand and a lasso fastened to his saddle. He charged him, struck him with his spear, and cut the fastenings of his cuirass. But Rustem, reaching out his hand, caught hold of Kaloun's spear, tore it from him, and struck him out of his saddle with it. Then as he lay upon the ground, he made Raksh trample on him till his brains were trodden out of his skull. When the Tartars saw their chief treated in this fashion, they turned their backs and fled.

Rustem and the King rode on till they came to Zal. Seven days they feasted and took counsel with the nobles, and on the eighth day Keïkobad was crowned King of Persia.

A few days afterwards the Persian army marched against the Tartars, and joined battle with them. When the conflict had lasted for some time, Rustem said to his father, "Tell me, my father, where is that villainous Prince, Afrasiab? What dress does he wear? Where does he set up his standard? Yonder I see a bright violet flag; is it his?"

"My son," said Zal, "listen to me. This Tartar Afrasiab is as strong and as fierce as a dragon. Beware of him. His flag is black; his coat of mail is black, and he has an iron badge on his arm. His armour is of iron embossed with gold; and he has a black plume on his helmet."

Rustem answered, "Have no fear on my account. I will catch him by the girdle, and drag him hither with his face upon the earth."

So saying he set spurs to Raksh. Afrasiab saw him scouring the plain, and, astonished at his youth, said to his nobles, "Who is this dragon that has broken its chain? I do not know his name."

"It is the son of Zal, the son of San," said they. "Do you not see that he has the club of San in his hand?"

Afrasiab galloped in front of his army. When Rustem saw him, he pulled up his horse and put his club over his shoulder; but when Afrasiab came near him, he let it hang down from his saddle, and caught the Prince by the girdle; he wished to drag him out of his saddle, and carry him off as the prize of his day's fighting. But, what with the weight of the King and Rustem's strong arm, the leather of the girdle broke. Afrasiab fell head foremost to the ground, and his nobles made a ring round him. When Rustem saw that the King had escaped him in this fashion, he bit the back of his hand, and said, "Why did I not lay hold under the armpits and carry him off, girdle and all?"

Meanwhile Afrasiab had been mounted by his attendants on a swift horse, and had escaped by way of the desert, leaving his army to shift for itself. And indeed it fared ill that day. Zal and Mihrab, the Prince of Cabul, and all the Persians and their allies, did wonders of valour. Many they killed, and many they took prisoners. But there was no one who could be compared to Rustem, who slew with his own hand as many as a whole army might have slain.

Meanwhile Afrasiab rode with all speed to the court of the King his father.

"My father," he said, "there is among the Persian warriors a youth such as cannot be matched elsewhere. He saw my standard, and rushing upon me caught me from my saddle—you would have said that I weighed no more than a fly. By good fortune the buckle of my girdle broke, and I escaped by the help of my nobles. But I am as nothing in his hands, and yet you know that I have some courage and strength. I say then—make peace with the Persians; for this man there is no resisting. You thought that the war was nothing more than a game; but it is a game of which your army has had enough."

The King was astonished to hear the fierce Afrasiab speak words of wisdom. Forthwith he wrote a letter to Keïkobad. "There has been war enough," he said, "let us have peace. Let the Tartars keep to their borders and the Persians to theirs. Then the two nations shall have rest and happiness." This letter he sealed, and sent by a messenger to Keïkobad.

When the King had read it, he said : " It is

not I who was the first to raise my hand against
the Tartars. Afrasiab came across our border,
and killed Newder our king. Nevertheless, if
you repent of your misdeeds and desire peace,
I will not refuse it."

So peace was made between the Persians
and the Tartars.

CHAPTER V.

KING KEÏKOBAD died, and his son Kaoüs sat
upon his throne. At first he was a moderate
and prudent prince ; but finding his riches
increase, and his armies grow more and more
numerous, he began to believe that there was
no one equal to him in the whole world, and
that he could do what he would. One day as
he sat drinking in one of the chambers of his
palace, and boasting after his custom, a Genius,
disguised as a minstrel, came to the King's
Chamberlain, and desired to be admitted to the
Royal presence. " I came," he said, " from the
country of the Genii, and I am a sweet singer.
Maybe the King, if he was to hear me, would
give me a post in his court."

The Chamberlain went to the King, and said, "There is a minstrel at the gate; he has a harp in his hand, and his voice is marvellously sweet."

"Bring him up," said the King.

So they brought him in, and gave him a place among the musicians, and commanded that he should give them a trial of his powers. So the minstrel, after playing a prelude on his harp, sang a song of the land of the Genii.

"There is no land in all the world"—this was the substance of his song—"like Mazanderan, the land of the Genii. All the year round the rose blooms in its gardens and the hyacinth on its hills. It knows no heat nor cold, only an eternal spring. The nightingales sing in its thicket, and through its valleys wander the deer, and the water of its stream is as the water of roses, delighting the soul with its perfume. Of its treasures there is no end; the whole country is covered with gold and embroidery and jewels. No man can say that he is happy unless he has seen Mazanderan."

When the King heard this song, he immediately conceived the thought of marching against this wonderful country. Turning, therefore, to his warriors, he said : "We are given over to feasting ; but the brave must not suffer himself to rest in idleness. I am wealthier and, I doubt not, stronger than all the kings that have gone before me ; it becomes me also to surpass them in my achievements. We will conquer the Land of Genii."

The warriors of the King were little pleased to hear such talk from his lips. No one ventured to speak, but their hearts were full of trouble and fear, for they had no desire to fight against the Genii.

"We are your subjects, O King," they said, "and will do as you desire." But when they were by themselves, and could speak openly, they said one to another, " What a trouble is this that has come of our prosperous fortune! Unless by good fortune the King forgets in his cups this purpose of his, we and the whole country are lost. Jemshid, whom the Genii and the Peris and the very birds of the air used to obey, never ventured to talk in this fashion of Mazanderan, or to seek war against the Genii ; and Feridun, though he was the wisest of kings, and skilful in all magical arts, never cherished such a plan." So they sat, overwhelmed with anxiety.

At last one of them said, " My friends; there is only one way of escaping from this danger. Let us send a swift dromedary to Zal of the white hair, with this message: ' Though your head be covered with dust, do not stay to wash it, but come.' Perhaps Zal will give the King wise advice, and, telling him that this plan of his is nothing but a counsel of Satan, will persuade him to change his purpose. Otherwise we are lost, small and great."

The nobles listened to this advice, and sent a messenger to Zal, mounted on a swift dromedary.

When Zal heard what had happened, he said: " The King is self-willed. He has not yet felt either the cold or the heat of the world. He thinks that all men, great and small, tremble at his sword, and it must needs be that he learn better by experience. However, I will go; I will give him the best advice that I can. If he will be persuaded by me, it will be well; but if not, the way is open, and Rustem shall go with his army." All night long he revolved these matters in his heart. The next morning he went his way, and arrived at the court of the King.

The King received him with all honour, bade him sit by his side, and inquired how he had borne the fatigue of his journey, and of the welfare of Rustem, his son. Then Zal spoke—

" I have heard, my lord, that you are forming plans against the Land of the Genii. Will it please you to listen to me ? There have been mighty kings before you, but never during all my years, which now are many, has any one of them conceived in his heart such a design as this. This land is inhabited by Genii that are skilful in all magical arts. They can lay such bonds upon men that no one is able to hurt them. No sword is keen enough to cut them through ; riches and wisdom and valour are alike powerless against them. I implore you, therefore, not to waste your riches, and the riches of your country and the blood of your warriors, on so hopeless an enterprise."

The King answered, " Doubtless it is true that the kings my predecessors never ventured to entertain such a plan. But am I not superior to them in courage, in power, and wealth ?

Had they such warriors as you, and Rustem your son ? Do not think to turn me from my purpose. I will go against the country of these accursed magicians, and verily I will not leave one single soul alive in it, for they are an evil race. If you do not care to come with me, at least refrain from advising me to sit idle upon my throne."

When Zal heard this answer, he said : " You are the King, and we are your slaves. Whatever you ordain is right and just, and it is only by thy good pleasure that we breathe and move. I have said what was in my heart. All that remains now is to obey, and to pray that the Ruler of the world may prosper your counsels."

When he had thus spoken, Zal took leave of the King, and departed for his own country.

The very next day the King set out with his army for the Land of the Genii, and, after marching for several days, pitched his tent at the foot of Mount Asprus, and held a great revel all the night long with his chiefs. The next morning he said, " Choose me two thousand men who will break down the gates of Mazanderan with their clubs. And take care that when you have taken the city you spare neither young nor old, for I will rid the world of these magicians." They did as the King commanded, and in a short space of time the city, which was before the richest and most beautiful in the whole world, was made into a desert.

When the King of Mazanderan heard of these things he called a messenger, and said: "Go to the White Genius and say to him, 'The Persians have come with a great army and are destroying everything. Make haste and help me, or there will be nothing left to preserve.'"

The White Genius said, "Tell the King not to be troubled; I will see to these Persians."

That same night the whole army of King Kaoüs was covered with a wonderful cloud. The sky was dark as pitch, and there fell from it such a terrible storm of hailstones that no one could stand against them. When the next morning came, lo! the King and all that had not fled—for many fled to their own coun try—or been killed by the hailstones, were-blind. Seven days they remained terrified and helpless. On the eighth day they heard the voice, loud as a clap of thunder, of the White Genius.

" King," said he, " you coveted the land of Mazanderan, you entered the city, you slew and took prisoners many of the people; but you did not know what I could do. And now, see, you have your desire. Your lot is of your own contriving."

The White Genius then gave over the King and his companions to the charge of an army of twelve thousand Genii, and commanded that they should be kept in prison, and have just so much food given them as should keep them alive from day to day. Kaoüs, however, contrived to send by one of his warriors a message to Zal the White-haired, telling him of all the troubles that had come upon him. When Zal heard the news he was cut to the heart, and sent without delay for Rustem. " Rustem," said he, " this is no time for a man to eat and drink and take his pleasure. The King is in the hands of Satan, and we must deliver him. As for me, I am old and feeble; but you are of the age for war. Saddle Raksh, your horse, and set forth without a moment's delay. The White Genius must not escape the punishment of his misdeeds at your hands."

" The way is long," said Rustem ; "how shall I go ?"

" There are two ways," answered Zal, "and both are difficult and dangerous. The King went by the longer way. The other is by far the shorter, a two weeks' march and no more ; but it is full of lions and evil Genii, and it is surrounded by darkness. Still, I would have you go by it. God will be your helper ; and difficult as the way may be, it will have an end, and your good horse Raksh will accomplish it. And if it be the will of Heaven that you should fall by the hand of the White Genius, who can change the ordering of destiny ? Sooner or later, we must all depart, and death should be no trouble to him who has filled the earth with his glory."

" My father, I am ready to do your bidding," said Rustem. " Nevertheless, the heroes of old cared not to go of their own accord into the land of death ; and it is only he who is weary of life that throws himself in the way of a roaring lion. Still I go, and I ask for no nelp but from the justice of God. With that on my side I will break the charm of the magicians. The White Genius himself shall not escape me."

Rustem armed himself, and went on his way.

CHAPTER VI.

RUSTEM made such speed that he accomplished two days' journey in one. But at last, finding himself hungry and weary, and seeing that there were herds of wild asses in the plain which he was traversing, he thought that he would catch one of them for his meal, and rest for the night. So pressing his knees into his horse's side he pursued one of them. There was no escape for the swiftest beast when Rustem was mounted on Raksh, and in a very short time a wild ass was caught with the lasso. Rustem struck a light with a flint stone, and making a fire with brambles and branches of trees, roasted the ass and ate it for his meal. This done he took the bridle from his horse, let him loose to graze upon the plain, and prepared to sleep himself in a bed of rushes. Now in the middle of this bed of rushes was a lion's lair, and at the end of the first watch the lion came back, and was astonished to see lying asleep on the rushes a man as tall as an elephant, with a horse standing near him. The lion said to himself, " I must first tear the horse, and then the rider will be mine whenever I please." So he leapt at Raksh ; but the horse darted at him like a flash of fire, and struck him on the head with his fore-feet. Then he seized him by the back with his teeth, and battered him to pieces on the earth. When Rustem awoke and saw the dead lion, which indeed was of a monstrous size, he said to Raksh, "Wise beast, who bade you fight with a lion ? If you had fallen under his claws, how should I have carried to Mazanderan this cuirass and helmet, this lasso, my bow and my sword ?" Then he went to sleep again ; but awaking at sunrise, saddled Raksh and went on his way.

He had now to accomplish the most difficult part of his journey across a waterless desert, so hot that the very birds could not live in it. Horse and rider were both dying of thirst, and Rustem,

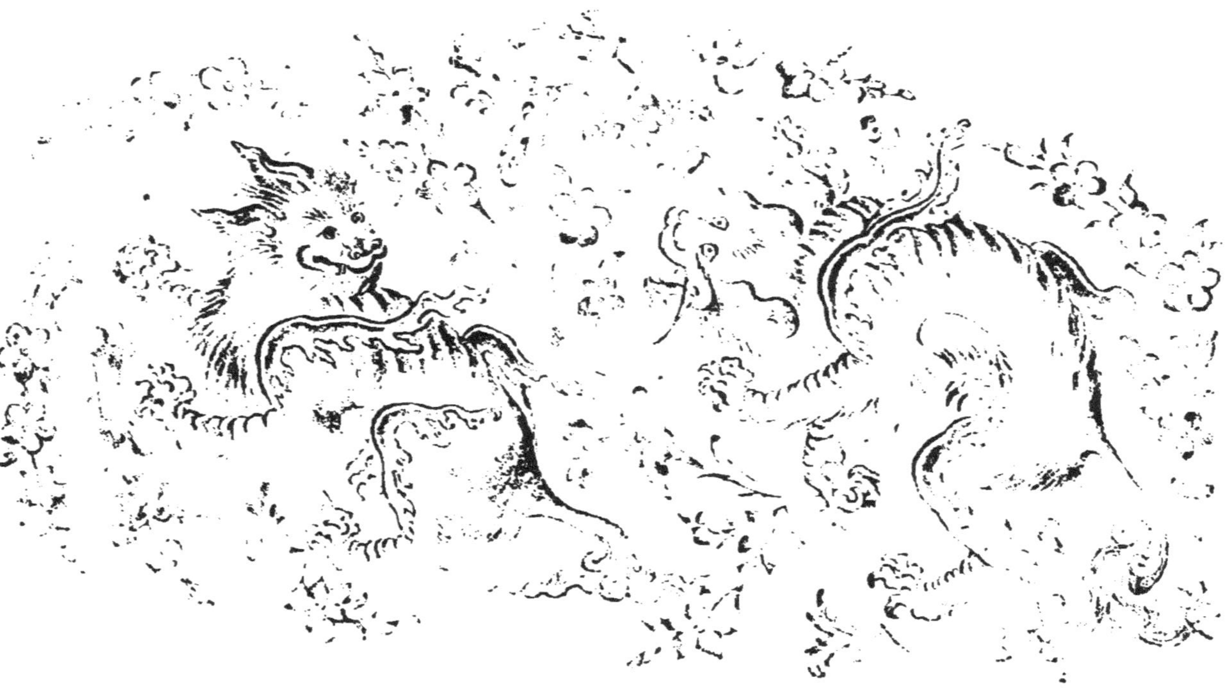

Monsters

dismounting, could scarcely struggle along while he supported his steps by his spear. When he had almost given up all hope, he saw a well-nourished ram pass by. "Where," said he to himself, "is the reservoir from which this creature drinks?" Accordingly he followed the ram's footsteps, holding his horse's bridle in one hand and his sword in the other, and the ram led him to a spring. Then Rustem lifted up his eyes to heaven and thanked God for His mercies; afterwards he blessed the ram, saying, "No harm come to thee for ever! May the grass of the valleys and the desert be always green for thee, and may the bow of him that would hunt thee be broken, for thou hast saved Rustem; verily without thee he would have been torn to pieces by the wild beasts of the desert."

After this he caught another wild ass, and roasted him for his meal. Then having bathed in the spring, he lay down to sleep; but before he lay down, he said to Raksh, his horse : " Do not seek quarrel or friendship with any. If an enemy come, run to me ; and do not fight either with Genius or lion."

After this he slept; and Raksh now grazed, and now galloped about over the plain.

Now it so happened that there was a great dragon that had its bed in this part of the desert. So mighty a beast was it, that not even a Genius had dared to pass by that way. The dragon was astonished to see a man asleep and a horse by his side, and began to make its way to the horse. Raksh did as he had been bidden, and running towards his master, stamped with his feet upon the ground. Rustem awoke, and seeing nothing when he looked about him—for the dragon meanwhile had disappeared—was not a little angry. He rebuked Raksh, and went to sleep again. Then the dragon came once more out of the darkness, and the horse ran with all speed to his master, tearing up the ground and kicking. A second time the sleeper awoke, but as he saw nothing but darkness round him, he was greatly enraged, and said to his faithful horse—

"Why do you disturb me? If it wearies you to see me asleep, yet you cannot bring the night to an end. I said that if a lion came to attack you, I would protect you; but I did not tell you to trouble me in this way. Verily, if you make such a noise again, I will cut off your head and go on foot, carrying all my arms and armour with me to Mazanderan."

A third time Rustem slept, and a third time the dragon came. This time Raksh, who did not venture to come near his master, fled over the plain; he was equally afraid of the dragon and of Rustem. Still his love for his master did not suffer him to rest. He neighed and tore up the earth, till Rustem woke up again in a rage. But this time God would not suffer the dragon to hide himself, and Rustem saw him through the darkness, and, drawing his sword, rushed at him.

But first he said—"Tell me your name; my hand must not tear your soul from your body before I know your name."

The dragon said—"No man can ever save himself from my claws; I have dwelt in this desert for ages, and the very eagles have not dared to fly across. Tell me then your name, bold man. Unhappy is the mother that bare you."

" I am Rustem, son of Zal of the white hair,"

said the hero, "and there is nothing on earth that I fear."

Then the dragon threw itself upon Rustem. But the horse Raksh laid back his ears, and began to tear the dragon's back with his teeth, just as a lion might have torn it.

The hero stood astonished for a while; then, drawing his sword, severed the monster's head from its body. Then, having first performed his ablutions, he returned thanks to God, and mounting on Raksh, went his way.

All that day he travelled across the plain, and came at sunset to the land of the magicians. Just as the daylight was disappearing, he spied a delightful spot for his night's encampment. There were trees and grass, and a spring of water. And beside the spring there was a flagon of red wine, and a roast kid, with bread and salt and confectionery neatly arranged. Rustem dismounted, unsaddled his horse, and looked with astonishment at the provisions thus prepared.   It was the meal of certain magicians, who had vanished when they saw him approach.

Of this he knew nothing, but sitting down without question, filled a cup with wine, and

Rustem slaying a Dragon.

taking a harp which he found lying by the side
of the flagon, sang—

> " The scourge of the wicked am I,
>   And my days still in battle go by;
>   Not for me is the red wine that glows
>   In the reveller's cup, nor the rose
>   That blooms in the land of delight;
>   But with monsters and demons to fight."

The music and the voice of the singer reached
the ears of a witch that was in those parts.
Forthwith, by her art, she made her face as fair
as spring, and, approaching Rustem, asked him
how he fared, and sat down by his side. The
hero thanked heaven that he had thus found in
the desert such good fare and excellent company
—for he did not know that the lovely visitor
was a witch. He welcomed her, and handed
her a cup of wine; but, as he handed it, he
named the name of God, and at the sound her
colour changed, and she became as black as
charcoal.

When Rustem saw this, quick as the wind he
threw his lasso over her head.

" Confess who you are," he cried; " show
yourself in your true shape."

Then the witch was changed into a decrepid, wrinkled old woman. Rustem cut her in halves with a blow of his sword.

The next day he continued his journey with all the speed that he could use, and came to a place where it was utterly dark. Neither sun, nor moon, nor stars could be seen ; and all that the hero could do was to let the reins fall on his horse's neck, and ride on as chance might direct.

In time he came to a most delightful country, where the sun was shining brightly, and where the ground was covered with green. Rustem took off his cuirass of leopard skin, and his helmet, and let Raksh find pasture where he could in the fertile fields, and lay down to sleep. When the keeper of the fields saw the horse straying among them and feeding, he was filled with rage, and running up to the hero, dealt him with his stick a great blow upon the feet.

Rustem awoke.

" Son of Satan," said the keeper, " why do you let your horse stray in the corn-fields ? "

Rustem leapt upon the man, and without uttering a single word good or bad, wrenched his ears from his head.

Now the owner of this fertile country was a young warrior of renown named Aulad. The keeper ran up to him with his ears in his hand, and said—

"There has come to this place a son of Satan, clad in a cuirass of leopard skin, with an iron helmet. I was going to drive his horse out of the corn-fields, when he leapt upon me, tore my ears from my head without saying a single word, and then lay down to sleep again."

Aulad was about to go hunting with his chiefs ; but when he heard the keeper's story he altered his plan, and set out to the place where he heard that Rustem had been seen. Rustem, as soon as he saw him approach, and a great company with him, ran to Raksh, leapt on his back, and rode forward. Aulad said to him, " Who are you ? What are you doing here ? Why did you pluck off my keeper's ears and let your horse feed in the corn-fields ? "

" If you were to hear my name," said Rustem, "it would freeze the blood in your heart."

So saying he drew his sword, and fastening his lasso to the bow of his saddle, rushed as a lion rushes into the midst of a herd of oxen.

With every blow of his sword he cut off a warrior's head, till the whole of Aulad's company was either slain or scattered. Aulad himself he did not kill, but throwing his lasso, caught him by the neck, dragged him from his horse, and bound his hands. "Now," said he, "if you will tell me the truth, and, without attempting to deceive, will show me where the White Genius dwells, and will guide me to where King Kaoüs is kept prisoner, then I will make you King of Mazanderan. But if you speak a word of falsehood you die."

"It is well," said Aulad; "I will do what you desire. I will show you where the King is imprisoned. It is four hundred miles from this place; and four hundred miles further, a difficult and dangerous way, is the dwelling of the White Genius. It is a cavern so deep that no mere man has ever sounded it, and lies between two mountains. Twelve thousand Genii watch it during the night, for the White Genius is the chief and master of all his tribe. You will find him a terrible enemy, and, for all your strong arms and hands, your keen sword, your lance and your club, you will scarcely be able to conquer him ;. and when you have conquered him, there will still be much to be done. In the city of the King of Mazanderan there are thousands of warriors, and not a coward among them ; and besides these, there are two hundred war-elephants. Were you made of iron, could you venture to deal alone with these sons of Satan ? "

Rustem smiled when he heard this, and said, " Come with me, and you will see what a single man, who puts his trust in God, can do. And now show me first the way to the King's prison."

CHAPTER VII.

RUSTEM mounted on Raksh, and rode gaily forward, and Aulad ran in front of him. For a whole day and night he ran, nor ever grew tired, till they reached the foot of Mount Asprus, where King Kaoüs had fallen into the power of the Genii. About midnight they heard a great beating of drums, and saw many fires blaze up.

Rustem said to Aulad, "What mean these fires that are blazing up to right and left of us ?"

Aulad answered, "This is the way into Mazanderan. The great Genius Arzeng must be there."

Then Rustem went to sleep; and when he woke in the morning he took his lasso and fastened Aulad to the trunk of a tree. Then hanging his grandfather's club to his saddle-bow, he rode on.

His conflict with Arzeng, the chief of the army of the Genii, was soon finished. As he approached the camp he raised his battle cry. His shout was loud enough, one would have said, to split the very mountains, and Arzeng, when he heard it, rushed out of his tent. Rustem set spurs to his horse, and galloping up to the Genius, caught him by the head, tore it from the body, and threw it into the midst of the army. When the Genii saw it, and caught sight also of the great club, they fled in the wildest confusion, fathers trampling upon their sons in their eagerness to escape. The hero put the whole herd of them to the sword, and then returned as fast as he could to the place where he had left Aulad bound to the tree. He unloosed the knots of the lasso, and bidding him lead the way to the prison-house of the King, set spurs to Raksh, Aulad running in front as before.

When they entered the town, Raksh neighed. His voice was as loud as thunder, and the King heard it, and in a moment understood all that had happened. "That is the voice of Raksh," he said to the Persians that were with him;

"our evil days are over. This was the way in which he neighed in King Kobad's time, when he made war on the Scythians."

The Persians said to themselves, "Our poor King has lost his senses, or he is dreaming. There is no help for us." But they had hardly finished speaking when the hero appeared, and did homage to the King. Kaoüs embraced him, and then said : " If you are to help me, you must go before the Genii know of your coming. So soon as the White Genius shall hear of the fall of Arzeng, he will assemble such an army of his fellows as shall make all your pains and labour lost. But you must know that you have great difficulties to overcome. First, you must cross seven mountains, all of them occupied by troops of Genii; then you will see before you a terrible cavern—more terrible, I have heard say, than any other place in the world. The entrance to it is guarded by warrior Genii, and in it dwells the White Genius himself. He is both the terror and the hope of his army. Conquer him, and all will be well. A wise physician tells me that the only remedy for my blindness is to drop into my eyes three drops of the White

Genius' blood. Go and conquer, if you would save your King."

Without any delay Rustem set forth, Raksh carrying him like the wind. When he reached the great cavern, he said to Aulad, who had guided him on his way as before, " The time of conflict is come. Show me the way."

Aulad answered, " When the sun shall grow hot, the Genii will go to sleep. That will be your time to conquer them."

Rustem waited till the sun was at its highest, and then went forth to battle. The Genii that were on guard fled at the sound of his voice, and he went on without finding any to resist him till he came to the great cavern of which the King had spoken. It was a terrible place to see, and he stood for a while with his sword in his hand, doubting what he should do. No one would choose such a spot for battle, and as for escaping from it, that was beyond all hope. Long he looked into the darkness, and at last he saw a monstrous shape which seemed to reach across the whole breadth of the cave. It was the White Genius that was lying asleep. Rustem did not attempt to surprise him in his sleep, but woke him by shouting his battle cry. When the White Genius saw him he rushed at once to do battle with him. First he caught up from the ground a stone as big as a mill-stone and hurled it at him. For the first time Rustem felt a thrill of fear, so terrible was his enemy. Nevertheless, gathering all his strength, he struck at him a great blow with his sword and cut off one of his feet. The monster, though having but one foot, leapt upon him like a wild elephant, and seized him by the breast and arms, hoping to throw him to the ground, and tore from his body great morsels of flesh, so that the whole place was covered with blood. Rustem said to himself, "If I escape to-day I shall live for ever;" and the White Genius thought, "Even if I do deliver myself from the claws of this dragon, I shall never see Mazanderan again." Still he did not lose courage, but continued to struggle against the hero with all his might.

So the two fought together, the blood and sweat running from them in great streams. At last Rustem caught the Genius round the body, and, putting out all his strength, hurled

Rustem slaying the White Genius.

him to the ground with such force that his soul
was driven out of his body. Then he plunged
his poniard into the creature's heart, and tore
the liver out of his body. This done he
returned to Aulad, whom he had left bound
with his lasso, loosed him, and set out for the
place where he had left the King. But first
Aulad said to him, " I have the marks of your
bonds upon me; my body is bruised with the
knots of your lasso; I beseech you to respect
the promise which you made me of a reward.
A hero is bound to keep his word."

Rustem said : " I promised that you should
be King of Mazanderan, and King you shall be.
But I have much to do before my word can be
kept. I have a great battle to fight, in which I
may be conquered, and I must rid this country
of the magicians with whom it is encumbered.
But be sure that, when all is done, I will not
fail of the promises which·I have made."

So Rustem returned to King Kaoüs, and,
dropping the blood of the White Genius into
his eyes, gave him back his sight. Seven days
the King and his nobles feasted together,
Rustem having the chief place. On the

eighth day they set out to clear the country of the accursed race of magicians. When they had done this, the King said, "The guilty have now been punished. Let no others suffer. And now I will send a letter to the King of Mazanderan."

So the King wrote a letter in these words: "You see how God has punished the wrong-doers—how He has brought to nought the Genii and the Magicians. Quit then your town, and come here to pay homage and tribute to me. If you will not, then your life shall be as the life of Arzeng and the White Genius."

This letter was carried to the King by a certain chief named Ferbad. When the King had read it he was greatly troubled. Three days he kept Ferbad as his guest, and then sent back by him this answer: "Shall the water of the sea be equal to wine? Am I one to whom you can say, 'Come down from your throne, and present yourself before me'? Make ready to do battle with me, for verily I will bring upon the land of Persia such destruction that no man shall be able to say what is high and what is low."

Ferbad hastened back to the King of Persia. "The man," he said, "is resolved not to yield." Then the King sent to Rustem. And Rustem said, "Send me with a letter that shall be as keen as a sword and a message like a thunder-cloud." So the King sent for a scribe, who, making the point of his reed as fine as an arrow-head, wrote thus: "These are foolish words, and do not become a man of sense. Put away your arrogance, and be obedient to my words. If you refuse, I will bring such an army against you as shall cover your land from one sea to the other; and the ghost of the White Genius shall call the vultures to feast on your brains."

The King set his seal to this letter, and Rustem departed with it, with his club hanging to his saddle-bow. When the King of Mazanderan heard of his coming, he sent some of his nobles to meet him. When Rustem saw them, he caught a huge tree that was by the wayside in his hands, twisted it with all his might, and tore it up roots and all. Then he poised it in his hand as if it were a javelin. One of the nobles, the strongest of them all, rode up to him, caught one of his hands, and pressed it with all his might. Rustem only smiled; but when in his turn he caught the noble's hand in his, he crushed all the veins and bones, so that the man fell fainting from his horse.

When the King heard what had been done, he called one of his warriors, Kalahour by name, the strongest man in his dominions, and said to him, "Go and meet this messenger; show him your prowess, and cover his face with shame." So Kalahour rode to meet Rustem, and, taking him by the hand, wrung it with all the strength of an elephant. The hand turned blue with the pain, but the hero did not flinch or give any sign of pain. But when in his turn he wrung the hand of Kalahour, the nails dropped from it as the leaves drop from a tree. Kalahour rode back, his hand hanging down, and said to the King, " It will be better for you to make peace than to fight with this lion, whose strength is such that no man can stand against him. Pay this tribute, and we will make it good to you. Otherwise we are lost."

At this moment Rustem rode up. The

King gave him a place at his right hand, and asked him of his welfare. Rustem, for answer, gave him the letter of Keï-Kaous. When the King had read the letter, his face became black as thunder. Then he said, "Carry back this answer to your master: 'You are lord of Persia, and I of Mazanderan. Be content; seek not that which is not yours. Otherwise your pride will lead you to your fall.'"

The King would have given Rustem royal gifts, robes of honour, and horses, and gold. But the hero would have none of them, but went away in anger. When he had returned to the King of Persia, he said to him, "Fear nothing, but make ready for battle. As for the warriors of this land of Mazanderan, they are nothing; I count them no better than a grain of dust."

Meanwhile the King of the Magicians prepared for war. He gathered an army, horsemen and foot-soldiers and elephants, that covered the face of the earth, and approached the borders of Persia; and, on the other hand, King Kaoüs marshalled his men of war and went out to encounter him. The King himself took his place in the centre of the line of battle, and in front of all stood the great Rustem.

One of the nobles of Mazanderan came out of their line, with a great club in his hands, and approaching the Persian army, cried in a loud voice, "Who is ready to fight with me? He should be one who is able to change water into dust."

None of the Persian nobles answered him, and King Kaoüs said, "Why is it, ye men of war, that your faces are troubled, and your tongues silent before this Genius."

But still the nobles made no answer. Then Rustem caught the rein of his horse, and, putting the point of his lance over his shoulder, rode up to the King, and said, "Will the King give me permission to fight with this Genius?"

The King said, "The task is worthy of you, for none of the Persians dare to meet this warrior. Go and prosper!"

So Rustem set spurs to Raksh, and rode against the warrior who had challenged the Persians.

"Hear," he said, as soon as he came near,

"your name is blotted out of the list of the living ; for the moment is come when you shall suffer the recompense of all your misdeeds."

The warrior answered, " Boast not yourself so proudly. My sword makes mothers childless."

When Rustem heard this he cried with a voice of thunder, " I am Rustem !" and the warrior, who had no desire to fight the champion of the world, turned his back and fled. But Rustem pursued him, and thrust at him with his lance where the belt joins the coat of mail, and pierced him through, for the armour could not turn the point of the great spear. Then he lifted him out of his saddle, and raised him up in the air, as if he were a bird which a man had run through with a spit. This done, he dashed him down dead upon the ground, and all the nobles of Mazanderan stood astonished at the sight.

After this the two armies joined battle. The air grew dark, and the flashing of the swords and clubs flew like the lightning out of a thunder-cloud, and the mountains trembled with the cries of the combatants. Never had any living man seen so fierce a fight before.

For seven days the battle raged, and neither the one side nor the other could claim the victory. On the eighth day King Kaoüs bowed himself before God, taking his crown from his head, and prayed with his face to the ground, saying, "O Lord God, give me, I beseech Thee, the victory over the Genii who fear Thee not."

Then he set his helmet on his head, and put himself at the head of his army. First of all Rustem began the attack, charging the centre of the enemy's army. He directed his course straight to the place where the King of Mazanderan stood, surrounded with his chiefs and a great host of elephants. When the King saw the shine of his lance, he lost courage, and would have fled. But Rustem, with a cry like a lion's roar, charged him, and struck him on the girdle with his spear. The spear pierced the steel, and would have slain the King, but that by his magic art he changed himself, before the eyes of all the Persian army, into a mass of rock. Rustem stood astonished to see such a marvel.

When King Kaoüs came up with his warriors, he said to Rustem, "What is it?

What ails you that you tarry here, doing nothing ?"

" My lord," answered Rustem, " I charged the King of Mazanderan, spear in hand; I struck him on the girdle, but when I thought to see him fall from his saddle, he changed himself into a rock before my eyes, and now he feels nothing that I can do."

Then King Kaoüs commanded that they should take up the rock and put it before his throne. But when the strongest men in the army came to handle the rock, or sought to draw it with cords, they could do nothing; it remained immovable. Rustem, however, without any one to help him, lifted it from the earth, and carrying it into the camp, threw it down before the King's tent, and said, " Give up these cowardly tricks and the art of magic. Else I will break this rock into pieces."

When the King of Mazanderan heard this, he made himself visible, black as a thunder-cloud, with a helmet of steel upon his head, and a coat of mail upon his breast. Rustem laughed, and caught him by the hand, and brought him before the King.

" See," said he, " this lump of rock, who, for fear of the hatchet, has given himself up to me!"

When Kaoüs looked at him and observed how savage of aspect he was, with the neck and tusks of a wild boar, he saw that he was not worthy to sit upon a throne, and bade the executioner take him away and cut him in pieces. This done, he sent to the enemies' camp, and commanded that all the spoil, the King's throne, and his crown and girdle, the the horses and the armour, the swords and jewels, should be gathered together. Then he called up his army, and distributed to them rewards in proportion to what they had done and suffered. After this he spent seven days in prayer, humbling himself before God, and offering up thanksgiving. On the eighth day he seated himself on his throne, and opened his treasures, and gave to all that had need. Thus he spent another seven days. On the fifteenth day, he called for wine and cups of amber and rubies, and sat for seven days on his throne, with the wine-cup in his hand.

He sent for Rustem, and said, " It is of your

doing, by your strength and courage, that I have recovered my throne."

Rustem answered, "A man must do his duty. As for the honours that you would give me, I owe them all to Aulad, who has always guided me on the right way. He hopes to be made King of Mazanderan. Let the King, therefore, if it please him, invest him with the crown."

And this the King did.

The next day Kaoüs and his army set out to return to the land of Persia. When he had reached his palace, he seated himself upon his throne, and sending for Rustem, put him at his side.

Rustem said, "My lord, permit me to go back to the old man Zal, my father."

The King commanded that they should bring splendid presents for the hero. The presents were these: A throne of turquoise, adorned with rams' heads; a royal crown set about with jewels; a robe of brocade of gold such as is worn by the King of Kings; a bracelet and a chain of gold; a hundred maidens, with faces fair as the full moon, and girdles of gold ; a hundred youths, whose hair was fragrant with musk; a hundred horses, caparisoned with gold and silver; a hundred mules with black hair, with loads of brocade that came from the land of Room and from Persia. After these they brought and laid at the hero's feet a hundred purses filled with gold pieces ; a cup of rubies, filled with pure musk ; another cup of turquoise, filled with attar of roses ; and, last of all, a letter written on pages of silk in ink made of wine and aloes and amber and the black of lamps. By this letter the King of Kings gave anew to Rustem the kingdom of the South. Then Kaoüs blessed him, and said : " May you live as long as men shall see the sun and the moon in heaven ! May the great of the earth join themselves to you ! May your own soul be full of modesty and tenderness ! "

Rustem prostrated himself on the earth, and kissed the throne ; and so took his departure.

CHAPTER VIII.

SOHRAB.

One day Rustem thought that he would hunt. So he filled his quiver with arrows, and, mounting his horse Raksh, set out for the country which borders on Tartary. As he went he came upon a plain which was covered with herds of wild asses. Rustem smiled to see them, and, pursuing them on his fleet-footed horse, killed many of them, some with his arrows, and some, first catching them with his lasso, with his club. His hunting done, he lighted a great fire of brushwood, brambles, and branches of trees; then taking a young tree to serve him for a spit, ran it through the body of one of the asses, and roasted the flesh at the fire. When it was well done, he tore it joint from joint, ate his full of it, and broke the bones for the marrow. His meal finished, he lay down to sleep, while Raksh grazed on the plain. While he slept, seven Tartar warriors came that way, and saw the tracks of Raksh, who had wandered far away from his master's camping-place. Not long afterwards they came upon him, and made haste to possess themselves of him. First they tried to throw a lasso over him, but when Raksh saw the lasso he rushed at them like a lion, struck two of them dead with two blows of his fore-feet, and bit off the head of a third. Thus three of the company were dead, and the brave Raksh was not yet taken. Nevertheless the other four entangled him with their lassos, and, so capturing him, took him with them to the town.

When Rustem woke from his sleep, he looked about for his horse, but could find no traces of him. "How can I go," he said to himself, "carrying my quiver and my club, this heavy helmet, this sword, and this coat of mail? The Tartars will say, 'Rustem slept and some one stole his horse,' and I shall be covered with shame."

When he came near to the town of Semengan, the King and his nobles saw that it was Rustem that was approaching. The King went out to meet him, and said: "What has happened? How is it that you came on foot? Tell us how we can serve you. We are all at your bidding."

Rustem saw that they were friends, and answered: "My horse Raksh has escaped from me on this plain without bit or reins. Find him for me, and I will reward you as is fitting. But if Raksh is not found, I will make many suffer for it."

The King said: "No one will dare to do you a wrong in this matter. Come and be my guest. Let us drive away care with the wine-cup. Anger profits nothing. It is by charming that one brings the serpent out of his hole. As for the horse Raksh, it is not possible that he should be hid, for all the world knows of him. We will look for him, and bring him to you without delay."

So Rustem put away all suspicion out of his mind, and became the guest of the King. So they sat and drank wine together, and the King waited upon him as though he were his slave.

While the hero tarried in the palace, the King's daughter, who had often heard of his prowess and courage, and of the great exploits which he had done, saw him and loved him. She was the most beautiful of maidens. Her eyebrows were arched, the two plaits of her hair like the ropes of a lasso, her lips like rubies, and she was tall as a cypress.

Rustem asked her in marriage of her father, and the King, who was glad to find so noble a husband for her, gladly listened to his suit. So the two—the maiden's name was Tehmina—were married with much rejoicing.

When the time came that Rustem must leave the King's court—for there were grave matters that called him back to Persia—he took an onyx bracelet that he wore upon his arm, and gave it to his wife, saying, " If God should give you a daughter, fasten this bracelet under the curls of her hair. But if you should bear a son, let him wear it on his arm, as his father has worn it."

So Rustem departed, taking his horse with him, for the King had found Raksh.

In due time Tehmina bore a son. The

infant was as beautiful as the moon. When
he was but a month old he had the limbs of a
yearling child ; at three years he learnt exer-
cises of arms ; at five he was as bold as a lion ;
and at ten there was not a man in the whole
country that dared wrestle with him. One day
he went to his mother, and said, " Tell me who
I am. What must I say when they ask me
my father's name ? "

Tehmina said, " You are the son of Rustem.
Never since God made the world has there
been such a warrior as he ; " and she showed
him a letter from Rustem, and three rubies
which he had sent for a gift. " But," she said,
" King Afrasiab must know nothing of this, for
he is the sworn foe of Rustem. He would kill
the son because he hates the father. And
besides, if your father knew to what strength
and stature you are grown, he would send for you,
and your mother's heart would break for grief."

Sohrab said—for that was the youth's name :
" This is a story that cannot be hid. But
listen to what I will do. I will put myself at
the head of an innumerable army of Tartars.
I will deprive King Kaoüs of his kingdom. I

will set Rustem upon his throne ; and, this done, I will make war against Afrasiab and possess myself of his throne. Seeing that Rustem is my father and I am his son, I will not suffer that there should be any kings in the world but he and I."

Sohrab, after he had chosen for himself a horse, having the good fortune to find one that was of the breed of Raksh, asked his grandfather to help him. " I would go," he said, " to the land of Persia, and help my father."

The King loaded him with gifts, and sent him away.

Meanwhile it was told to King Afrasiab that Sohrab was gathering an army againt the King of Persia. He called his nobles and said : " Listen to me ; I have a plan which shall rid us of our enemies. Rustem must not know that Sohrab is his son. The two will meet in battle, and it may be that the young lion will kill the old one. If it be so, one day we will take Sohrab by stratagem and slay him. But if Rustem, on the other hand, should slay his son, then his heart will be eaten away with grief, and we need fear him no more."

Accordingly Afrasiab sent messengers to Sohrab with gifts and this message : " You will do well if you can conquer the land of Persia. I send you for your help such an army as is fitting. Go on, and prosper."

So Sohrab set out with his army. He came in his march to a certain stronghold that was called the White Fort, and was the chief hope of the Persians. The governor of the fort was an old man and very feeble ; but in the garrison there was a very brave champion, Hedjir by name, who, when he saw the army of Sohrab approaching, rushed out to meet him. "Come to me," he said, in his pride, " and I will cut your head from your body, and give your flesh to the vultures to eat."

Sohrab smiled to hear such brave words, and charged his enemy. The two met. Hedjir struck Sohrab on the girdle with a spear, but the point did not pierce the armour. But Sohrab, reversing his spear, struck Hedjir with the shaft, and felled him from his saddle ; then, leaping from his horse, stood over him, and would have cut his head from his body, but that the vanquished man begged for quarter.

Sohrab granted him his life, bound him with cords, and sent him a prisoner to the King.

The old governor of the fort had a daughter, Gurdafurd by name, a very fair maiden, but as strong and brave as any warrior in the land. It troubled her greatly to see the young champion discomfited and bound, and without hesitating a moment she armed herself, hid her long hair under her helmet, and rode forth from the fort to do battle with the Tartars.

She rode in front of the army of the besiegers, and said, "Who is there among you that will come and fight with me?" None of them were willing to accept her challenge; but when Sohrab saw her he said, "Here is another wild ass for my lasso!" and hastily putting on his armour rode out to meet her. The girl let fly a storm of arrows at him, attacking him first from one side then from the other; and when Sohrab charged her, threw her bow over her shoulder, put her spear in rest, and galloped to meet him. Sohrab drew his spear back so far that the point was almost level with his body; then, delivering it with all his force, struck Gurdafurd on the girdle, burst the

fastenings of her coat of mail, and hurled her
from her saddle like a ball struck by a racquet.
The girl twisted herself under her saddle, drew
a sword from her girdle, and cut Sohrab's spear
in half. Then she jumped again into the saddle,
but turned to fly, for she had little liking for
the conflict. Sohrab slackened the reins of his
horse, and, galloping after her at full speed,
overtook her, and catching her by the helmet,
drew it from her head. Then all her long hair
fell down, and the young hero knew that he
had been fighting with a girl. "Well!" said
he, "if the maidens of Persia fight in this
fashion, the men must be notable warriors."
He threw his lasso round her waist, and said,
"Do not attempt to escape; but tell me, beautiful girl, why did you seek this conflict?"

The girl said, "All the army will laugh at
you, if they should see my face and my hair.
They will say, 'The brave Sohrab went out
to fight a woman.' Let us conceal this adven-
ture. The fort is yours, and all the soldiers
in it and all the treasure, as soon as you shall
be pleased to take possession of it."

Sohrab said, "Do not fail of your promise,

and do not trust in the strength of your walls. Were they as high as the vault of heaven, my club would level them to the ground."

So they rode together to the gate of the fort, and Gurdafurd, wounded and wearied, dragged herself within.   Her father received her with great joy, and said, " You have done well, my daughter.   We have no cause to be ashamed of your courage and address.   Thanks be to God, who has not suffered this stranger to kill you."

After this the girl mounted on the wall, and seeing Sohrab waiting beneath, said to him, " Why do you weary yourself with waiting, lord of the Tartars?   Return to the place whence you came."

Sohrab said : " Treacherous one! I swear by heaven and earth that you will repent of this falsehood.   Where is the treaty that you made with me, that you would deliver up the fort, with all its garrison and its treasure ? "

The girl laughed, and said: " Take care ; the great Rustem will soon be here, and not a man of your army will be left alive.   But what a pity that such arms and such a breast as yours should be a prey for jackals! Pride yourself as you will on your strength, but yet the stupid cow will eat the grass upon your grave."

Sohrab was covered with shame to hear these mocking words. But he said, "It is too late to give battle to-day; but with dawn to-morrow we will lay the fort level with the dust." Then he shook the reins of his horse, and galloped back to the camp.

At dawn he marched against the fort with his army. But there was no one to be seen upon the walls. He rode up to the gate, and it was opened to him. But there was not a single armed man in the whole place. In fact, the governor and the garrison had departed in the night by a passage under the earth, of which no one was aware, and with them was gone the beautiful Gurdafurd. This troubled Sohrab more than anything else, for his heart was full of love for the girl, so beautiful and so brave.

CHAPTER IX.

MEANWHILE the governor of the fort had sent a letter to King Kaoüs, telling him how there had appeared among the Tartars a mighty champion, against whom, such was the strength of his arms, no one could stand; how he had overthrown and taken prisoner their champion, and now threatened to overrun and conquer the whole land of Persia. When the King had received and read this letter he was greatly troubled, and, calling a scribe, said to him, "Sit down and write a letter to Rustem." So the scribe sat down and wrote. The letter was this: "There has appeared among the Tartars a great champion, strong as an elephant and fierce as a lion. No one can stand against him. We look to you for help. It is of your doing that our warriors hold their heads so high. Come, then, with all the speed that you can use so soon as you shall have read this letter. Be it night or day, come at once; do not open your mouth to speak; if you have a bunch of roses in your hand do not stop to smell it, but come; for the warrior of whom I write is such that you only can meet him."

King Kaoüs sealed the letter and gave it to a warrior named Giv. At the same time he said, "Haste to Rustem. Tarry not on the way; and when you are come, do not rest there for an hour. If you arrive in the night, depart again the next morning." So Giv departed, and travelled with all his speed, allowing himself neither sleep nor food. When he approached Zabulistan, the watchman said, "A warrior comes from Persia, riding like the wind." So Rustem, with his chiefs, went out to meet him. When they had greeted each other, they returned together to Rustem's palace. Giv delivered his message and handed the King's letter, telling himself much more that he had heard about the strength and courage of this Tartar warrior. Rustem heard him with astonishment, and said, " This champion is like, you say, to the great San, my grandfather. That such a man should come from the free Persians is possible ; but that he should be among those slaves the Tartars, is past belief. I have myself a child, whom the daughter of a Tartar king bore to me; but the child is a girl. This, then, that you tell me is passing strange ; but for the present let us make merry."

So they made merry with the chiefs that were assembled in Rustem's palace. But after awhile Giv said again: " King Kaoüs commanded me, saying, ' You must not sleep in Zabulistan ; if you arrive in the night, set out again the next morning. It will go ill with us if we have to fight before Rustem comes.' It is necessary, then, great hero, that we set out in all haste for Persia."

Rustem said, " Do not trouble yourself about this matter. We must all die some day. Let us, therefore, enjoy the present. Our lips are dry, let us wet them with wine. As to this Tartar, fortune will not always be with him. When he sees my standard, his heart will fail him."

So they sat, drinking the red wine and singing merry songs, instead of thinking of the King and his commands. The next day Rustem passed in the same fashion, and the third also. But on the fourth Giv made preparations to depart, saying to Rustem, " If we do not make haste to set out, the King will be wroth, and his anger is terrible." Rustem said, " Do not trouble yourself ; no man dares to be wroth with me." Nevertheless he bade them saddle Raksh, and set out with his companions.

When they came near the King's palace, a great company of nobles rode out to meet them, and conducted them to the King, and they paid their homage to him. But the King turned away from them in a rage. " Who is Rustem," he cried, " that he forgets his duty to me, and disobeys my commands? If I had a sword in my hand this moment, I would cut off his head, as a man cuts an orange in half. Take him, hang him up alive on gallows, and never mention his name again in my presence."

Giv answered, " Sir, will you lay hands upon Rustem ? "

The King burst out again in rage against Giv and Rustem, crying to one of his nobles, "Take these two villains and hang them alive on gallows." And he rose up from his throne in fury. The noble to whom he had spoken laid his hand upon Rustem, wishing to lead him out of the King's presence, lest Kaoüs in his rage should do him an injury. But Rustem cried out, "What a king are you! Hang this Tartar, if you can, on your gallows. Keep such things for your enemies. All the world has bowed itself before me and Raksh my horse. And you—you are king by my grace."

Thus speaking, he struck away the hand that the noble had laid upon him so fiercely that the man fell headlong to the ground, and he passed over his body to go from the presence of the King. And as he mounted on Raksh, he cried : "What is Kaoüs that he should deal with me in this fashion?   It is God who has given me strength and victory, and not he or his army. The nobles would have given me the throne of Persia long since, but I would not receive it ; I kept the right before my eyes.

Verily, had I not done so, you, Kaous, would not be sitting upon the throne." Then he turned to the Persians that stood by, and said, " This brave Tartar will come. Look out for yourselves how you may save your lives. Me you shall see no more in the land of Persia."

The Persians were greatly troubled to hear such words ; for they were sheep, and Rustem was their shepherd. So the nobles assembled, and said to each other : " The King has forgotten all gratitude and decency. Does he not remember that he owes to Rustem his throne—nay, his very life ? If the gallows be Rustem's reward, what shall become of us ? "

So the oldest among them came and stood before the King, and said : " O King, have you forgotten what Rustem has done for you and for this land—how he conquered Mazanderan and its king and the White Genius; how he gave you back the sight of your eyes ? And now you have commanded that he should be hanged alive upon a gallows. Are these fitting words for a king ? "

The King listened to the old man, and said : " You speak well. The words of a king should be words of wisdom. Go now to Rustem, and speak good words to him, and make him forget my anger."

So the old man rode after Rustem, and many of the nobles went with him. When they had overtaken him, the old man said, "You know that the King is a wrathful man, and that in his rage he speaks hard words. But you know also that he soon repents. But now he is ashamed of what he said. And if he has offended, yet the Persians have done no wrong that you should thus desert them."

Rustem answered, "Who is the King that I should care for him? My saddle is my throne, my helmet is my crown, my corselet is my robe of state. What is the King to me but a grain of dust? Why should I fear his anger? I delivered him from prison; I gave him back his crown. And now my patience is at an end."

The old man said, "This is well. But the King and his nobles will think, 'Rustem fears this Tartar,' and they will say, 'If Rustem is afraid, what can we do but leave our country?' I pray you therefore not to turn your back upon the King, when things are in such a plight. Is it well that the Persians should become the slaves of the infidel Tartars ?"

Rustem stood confounded to hear such words. " If there were fear in my heart, then I would tear my soul from my body. But you know that it is not ; only the King has treated me with scorn."

But he perceived that he must yield to the old man's advice. So he went back with the nobles.

As soon as the King saw him, he leapt upon his feet, and said, " I am hard of soul, but a man must grow as God has made him. My heart was troubled by the fear of this new enemy. I looked to you for safety, and you delayed your coming. Then I spoke in my wrath ; but I have repented, and my mouth is full of dust."

Rustem said, " It is yours to command, O King, and ours to obey. You are the master, and we are your slaves. I am but as one of those who open the door for you, if indeed I am worthy to be reckoned among them. And now I am come to execute your commands."

Kaoüs said, " It is well.   Now let us feast. To-morrow we will prepare for war."

So Kaoüs, and Rustem, and the nobles feasted till the night had passed and the morning came.

CHAPTER X.

THE next day King Kaoüs and Rustem, with a great army, began their march. Now Sohrab was still at the fort from which the beautiful Gurdafurd had escaped. When the army of the Persians came in sight, the Tartars that were in the fort set up a great shout; and Sohrab hearing it, came and stood on the rampart, with Hedjir, the champion whom he had conquered and taken prisoner, by his side. "You do not see," he said, "in this great army a man with a great club who would be able to meet me in battle. There are many men, it is true; but not a single man of war. Verily I will cover the plain with their blood, as the waters cover the sea."

So saying, he went down from the rampart,

and called for a cup of wine. He had not a thought of fear in his heart. On the other side, the King's army pitched their tents on the plain, which they covered from side to side with their encampment.

That night Rustem went to the King, and said, "Will the King suffer me to go out to-night without helmet or belt that I may see for myself who this champion is, and who are the warriors that follow him?"

The King said, "It is well thought of. Only be prudent, and may God have you in His keeping."

So Rustem put on the dress of a Tartar, and set out for the fort. He made his way into it, like a lion which steals on a herd of antelopes, and saw Sohrab and the chief sitting at the feast.

Now Sohrab's mother had said to Zendeh her brother, when her son was setting out for the war, "Go with Sohrab, for you know the face of Rustem; and when the time is come, you will show my son his father." So Sohrab sat at the feast, and Zendeh his uncle sat by him.

Rustem stood by the door watching the

feasters, and it so chanced that Zendeh, leaving the room, saw him standing there. "Who are you?" he said, for there was not a man in the whole army of the Tartars that was his like in strength and stature.

Rustem answered him not a word, but struck him on the nape of the neck so fierce a blow that he fell down and died. There was no more feasting or fighting for Zendeh.

When Sohrab saw that Zendeh's place remained empty, he asked where he was. Some of the guests went to look for him, and found him lying dead by the door. They came and told Sohrab, who called the nobles and said to them, "We must not sleep to-night, but must spend the time in sharpening the points of our lances. The wolf has come into the fold, and, in spite of shepherds and dogs, has taken the best of the flock. With God for my helper, I will avenge on the Persian the death of Zendeh."

When he had thus spoken he came back to his place, and cried, "Zendeh will be wanting by my side in the battle; but I am not weary of the feast."

Meanwhile Rustem went back to King Kaoüs, and told him what he had seen and done. "As for Sohrab," said he, "he has not his equal in Persia, or among the Tartars. He might have been the great warrior San, and what can I say more?"

The next day Sohrab put on his armour, and, going out of the fort, chose a steep place from which he could see the army of the Persians, and bade Hedjir come and stand by him. "Deal fairly with me," said he, "answer me true, and it shall go well with you. You shall have rewards to your heart's content. But if you deceive me, you shall lie in prison for the rest of your days."

Hedjir said, "I will tell you truly all that I can about the army of the Persians. And, indeed, why should I lie unto my lord?"

Sohrab went on, "I am going to ask you questions about the great men of the Persian army. Tell me now who they are. And first I see a tent of leopard skin, surrounded with brocade of many colours, and guarded by a hundred war-elephants. Over the tent there floats a violet flag, on which are figured the sun and the moon in gold. Whose is this tent?"

"That," said Hedjir, "is the tent of the Persian king."

"I see another tent," said Sohrab, "and the flag that flies over it has the figure of an elephant. Whose is it?"

"That is the tent of Thoüs, son of King Nereder."

"And now," Sohrab went on, "tell me whose is that tent of green? I see, sitting on a chair, a stalwart hero, with such an air, such shoulders, and such a frame as I have never seen before. Though he is sitting, yet he overtops all the warriors that are near him. And in front of him there stands a great charger, as high as the hero himself; and from the saddle there hangs a lasso. Nowhere have I seen such a man or such a horse. See his standard; it has the figure of a dragon, and on the spear-head is a lion's head."

Hedjir said to himself, " If I were to tell this young lion that this great warrior is Rustem, he would do his best to slay him. No; I will keep his name secret." So he said: 'This is one of the King's allies that is newly come from China."

"But what is his name?" said Sohrab.

"I do not know," answered the other, "for I was in the fort when he came to the King."

Sohrab was greatly grieved to find no trace of Rustem. His mother had told him certain signs by which he should know the hero. He saw them all, but he could not believe his eyes. Again he asked Hedjir about the green tent, and the mighty horse, and the lasso hanging from the saddle. But Hedjir answered: "Why should I hide the truth from you? If I do not tell you the name of this warrior from China, it is because I do not know it."

"But," said Sohrab, "where is Rustem? Not a word have you said of him; and yet so great a hero could not remain concealed in the middle of a camp. You told me that he is the chief of the army and the guardian of the provinces. Why, then, is he nowhere to be seen?"

Hedjir answered: "Perhaps he is gone to Zabulistan. It is now that they hold their feasts in the rose-gardens of that land."

"This is idle," said Sohrab. "Rustem is one

who will always be found in the front of the battle. Now, listen to me. If you will tell me which is Rustem, I will put you above all the people and load you with treasure. But if you hide from me what I want to know, I will cut your head from your body. Now choose between the two."

" Prince," said the other, " when you are tired of life, go out and fight with Rustem, who can kill two hundred men with one blow of his club."

Nevertheless he thought to himself : " If I show Rustem to this young lion he will rush on him and slay him, for all his strength and vigour. After this there is not a Persian who will dare to fight with him, and he will become King of Persia. No ; I will hide the truth, and if I die, I die." Then, turning to Sohrab, he said : " Why are you so angry, and why do you threaten to kill me because I do not point out Rustem to you ? But after all, are you not hiding your real thought ? You want to meet Rustem in battle ; but I say to you, Avoid him, for surely he will bring you to nought."

Sohrab, in a rage, struck him from his horse

to the ground. Then, going back to the fort, he armed himself for battle, and went out. First he charged the King's tent, and not one of the warriors of Persia dared to stand before him. He cried out to the King and said : " Noble King, what are you doing here on the field of battle? How dare you take the lance of Kaoüs, you who never dare to fight among the warriors in the battle. Listen to me. The night that Zendeh was slain I swore a great oath that I would not leave a man, little or great, alive in Persia, and that I would hang the King of Persia alive on a gallows. Come, now, if you have a champion who dares to meet me, let him come forth ! "

Not a man among the Persians took up this challenge; and the King, in great trouble, sent to Rustem, saying : " The faces of my warriors grow pale before this young Tartar, and there is not one who dares meet him in battle."

Rustem said to the messenger : "When other kings have called me, it has been sometimes to the battle and sometimes to the banquet; but King Kaoüs never calls me except to fight for him."

Nevertheless he bade his people saddle his horse Raksh, and he put on his circlet of leopard-skin and his royal girdle, and mounted, and set out for the battle, with his standard carried before him.

When he saw Sohrab, and observed how tall and stalwart he was, he cried out to him: "Come out from the line of your army, and I will come out from mine."

Sohrab rubbed his hands in delight, and rushed out, saying: "We are warriors, you and I. Do not call to your side any of the men of Persia, and there shall be no Tartar with me. You and I will fight alone. But listen: you cannot stand against me. You are tall of stature, and you have stalwart arms; but the weight of years is on you."

Rustem looked at the young man, and said: "Young man, the earth is dry and cold, but the air is sweet and warm. I have fought in many a battle; many an army have I put to flight; many a warrior and many a genius have I slain, and never yet have I been beaten. But I should be grieved to do you any harm. Leave these Tartars and come to us. I know not a man in the whole land of Persia who has arms and shoulders such as yours."

When Rustem thus spake, the heart of Sohrab went out to him, and he said: "Come, now; I will ask you a question, and I beseech you to answer me truly. Tell me frankly who you are. Surely you are Rustem, the son of Zal?"

Rustem answered: "It is false; I am not Rustem; I am but a common man; I have neither throne, nor palace, nor crown."

When Sohrab heard this his heart was filled with despair, and he addressed himself to the combat.

The two champions chose a narrow place, and attacked each other with short spears. And when their spears had no more iron left on them—so fierce were their blows—they drew their Indian swords, and fell to work again. And when their swords were broken they used their clubs. Terrible blows they dealt each other! The armour of their horses was broken in pieces; their coats of mail were shattered. At last neither the warriors nor their horses moved more, so fierce had been their struggle. Surely this was a strange and marvellous thing!

The beasts know their own young; but man in his fury cannot distinguish between his son and his enemy!

Rustem said to himself: "The battle with the White Genius was but child's play to this. Never yet have I been conquered, and now my heart fails me before this man without a name."

When the two combatants had rested awhile they renewed the battle. Rustem seized Sohrab by the belt, hoping to drag him from his saddle; but he could not move him an inch from his place. Then Sohrab took up again his great club from where it hung by the side of the saddle, and dealt Rustem a mighty blow that bruised his shoulder. The hero writhed under the agony, but was strong enough to swallow down the pain. But Sohrab saw that he had struck a timely stroke, and smiled, saying: "Warrior, you are not one who can stand against the blows of the strong. But it is your age that disables you; it is folly for the aged to match themselves with the young."

After this the two combatants parted, and Rustem chased the army of the Tartars, as a tiger rushes on his prey. When Sohrab saw this he fell, in his turn, upon the Persians, and scattered them like a flock of sheep before him.

Rustem was filled with fury at the sight, and cried: "Man of blood, why have you fallen on the Persians, like a wolf on the fold?"

Sohrab answered: "The army of the Tartars had not joined in the battle, and yet you charged it."

Rustem said: "We will fight again to-morrow, and God shall decide who of us two shall remain the conqueror."

After this they rode back each to his own army. Rustem sought the presence of the King, and told him what a mighty champion this Sohrab was. "We tried all our arms against each other," he said; "the arrow, the sword, the mace, and the lasso, but it was all in vain. At last I caught him by the girdle, hoping to lift him from his saddle, as I have done many a warrior before; but the wind might as well try to drag a mountain from its place as I drag this young warrior from his seat. Nevertheless, I will meet him again to-morrow, and then we will see what is the will of God, whether he is to prevail or I."

CHAPTER XI.

SOHRAB (*continued*).

THAT night Rustem said to his brother, "If I
fall to-morrow in the conflict, let all my army
depart from the field of battle and return to
Zabulistan, to the old man Zal. Console my
mother in her sorrow. Let her not bind her
heart for ever to the dead. I have no cause
to complain of fate. Many a lion, many a
warrior, many a Genius have I slain, many a
fortress have I taken, and I have never been
overcome. And say to Zal, my father, 'Be
faithful to the King, and obey his commands.'
As for me, let him remember that old and
young must die."

Sohrab passed the night feasting. He said
to one of his followers : " My heart goes out
to that brave warrior with whom I have fought

to-day. I see in him all the signs by which my mother told me I was to recognize my father, and my heart trembles. I must not fight against my father."

The man to whom he spoke said : "I have seen Rustem in battle, and his horse Raksh also I have seen; nor is the horse of this warrior unlike him. Nevertheless, he does not strike the earth with so heavy a tread."

The next day at dawn Sohrab put on his cuirass and his helmet and armed himself, and, mounting his horse, rode into the space between the two armies. And Rustem, on the other hand, rode out to meet him.

Sohrab spoke to Rustem with a smile upon his lips. One would have thought that they had spent the night together as friends at a feast. "How have you slept ?" he said. " How do you fare to-day ? Why is your heart bent on battle ? Put down your club and your sword. Let us sit together on the ground, and drive away our cares with the wine-cup. Wait till some one else shall come to do battle with you, but with me make a covenant of friendship, and tell me your name and your family. Surely you are Rustem, lord of Zabulistan, son of the white-haired Zal.

Rustem answered : " Young man, we are met here to fight ; I will not listen to your deceitful words.   No, we will do our best, you and I ; and the issue is with God."

Sohrab said : " Old man, I have spoken in vain.   I would have you die in your bed when your time shall come, and when these whom you have behind you shall prepare for your burial. But since you put your life in my hands, let us accomplish the purposes of God."

The two warriors then dismounted, and tying their chargers to the rocks, rushed upon each other.   Many a blow they struck, till they were both covered with blood and sweat.   And so they fought, without advantage to one or the other, from morning till noonday, and from noonday till the shadows began to lengthen upon the sand.   At last Sohrab, leaping like a lion, seized Rustem by the girdle, lifted him from the ground, and threw him down, his face and mouth covered with dust ; and he couched upon him, as a lion couches on a wild ass that he has caught.   Then he drew his dagger, and was about to cut his enemy's head from the body.

Rustem bethought him of a device by which he might save his life. "Young man," he said, "truly you know well how to manage the lasso and the club, the sword and the bow. But listen to me. Our customs of war are not as yours. If a warrior fights with another, and throws him, he does not cut his head from the body the first time; but if he throw him a second time, then he has right to do so. This is our custom of war."

The young man believed what the old warrior said, for he was of a generous heart; and also fate would have it so. So he let Rustem go free.

After a while came one of the Tartar warriors, and asked him how he had fared in the conflict. When Sohrab told him what had happened, and what Rustem had said, the man cried: "Alas! young man, are you weary of your life? You have let the lion, whom you had caught in your snare, escape. Beware of what will happen. It was a wise man who said, 'Despise no enemy, be he ever so weak,' and think what an enemy is this!"

Sohrab was sorry to hear these words, but

said : " Trouble not yourself ; I shall fight again to-morrow, and you shall see the yoke upon his neck once more." So saying he returned to the camp.

Rustem, on the other hand, when he rose from the ground, washed his face in a stream, and prayed to God to give him the victory, not knowing for what he prayed. It is said that Rustem's strength had once been such that when he put his feet upon a rock they would sink into it, and that he had prayed to God that a part of this strength might be taken from him. But now that he found himself in such danger, and was full of the fear of Sohrab, he prayed once more that his strength might be restored to him as it was before. And again he did not know for what he prayed.

When he had washed off the dust in the stream, he came back to the place of combat, and Sohrab also, seeing him return, left the camp. But when they met, and, laying hold of each other's belts, wrestled as before, then it seemed as if Sohrab had in a moment lost all his strength. Rustem seized him by the head and arm and bent him back, and so threw him on the ground. No thought had he of waiting till he should have thrown the young man a second time, but, knowing that he would not long remain where he lay, drew his sword from its scabbard, and plunged it into his breast.

Sohrab knew that he had received his death-blow. He said to Rustem : " This is my own doing, and it is chance that has put in your hand the key of my fate. My mother told me the signs by which I should know my father, and my love for him has led me to my death. I sought to see his face, and I have sought in vain. I shall never see it; and now I die. But as for you, were you to become a fish in the sea, or a star in the sky, my father will take vengeance on you when he shall hear that I am dead."

Rustem's heart sank in him when he heard these words. " Tell me," he cried, " what marks you have of Rustem. If this that you say be true, may his name perish for ever!" And he threw himself on the ground, and tore his hair with loud cries.

Sohrab said : " If it be so, if indeed you are Rustem, then it is of your own evil soul that you have killed me. Did I not seek by every means to make peace between us? And did I find one movement of tenderness in you? But open my cuirass, and look at what you will see. When my mother heard the sound of my trumpets at the gate, she ran to meet me, her cheeks red with weeping, and fastened a bracelet of onyx to my arm, and said, 'Keep this, it is a remembrance of your father; and use it when the time is come.' But alas! the time is come too late. We have fought together, and the son is dying before the father's eyes."

When Rustem had opened the cuirass, and saw the bracelet of onyx, he tore his garments and cried out in despair, and threw dust upon his head.

But Sohrab said: "There is no remedy. It was to be, and it is. What profits this grief?"

After a while he said again: "Now that I am about to die, the Tartars are in an evil case. Show, I pray you, your love for me, by hindering the King from marching against them. It was because they trusted in me, that they have invaded the land of Persia. Let them, therefore, return to their own country in peace.   And there is a prisoner in the camp ; I asked him about you, and he lied to me, denying the signs which I knew in my heart to be yours.   Nevertheless, see that he comes to no harm.   And as for me, I came like the thunder, and I go as the wind ; perhaps I shall meet you in heaven."

Rustem rode back to the army.   The Persians were glad to see him return alive; but when they perceived that his garments were torn and his head covered with dust, they asked him the cause.   " I have slain," he said, " the noblest of sons."

Thus Sohrab died by the hand of his father.

CHAPTER XII.

GUSTASP, King of Persia (he reigned second after Kaoüs), had a son whose name was Isfendiar, a very brave hero, who, among other exploits, had killed one of the great birds that are called Simorgs. Isfendiar was so proud of his victories that he conceived the idea of demanding the throne of Persia from his father. Accordingly he went to the King and said: "See what I have done: I have conquered the Tartars; I have brought their treasures into your palace; you promised that if I came back, having achieved so much, and came back in safety, you would deliver to me the throne and the royal crown. I pray you, therefore, to fulfil your promise."

Gustasp answered : " There is yet one enemy

to be subdued—Rustem, the son of Zal. This Rustem in former days was obedient to the Kings of Persia, now he holds himself to be their superior. Go, therefore, and conquer him, be it by stratagem or by force, and bring him bound before me, and I swear that I will surrender to you the throne."

His son said : "Ask anything else of me— that I should make war against the King of China, or against any other ruler under the sun ; but do not ask me to go against this old champion Rustem, the man who has defended for so long this realm of Persia."

The King said again : "Rustem has forgotten his duty to God and the King ; go, then, bind his hands, and bring him entangled in your lasso before me."

His son answered : "Sire, it is not of Rustem that you are thinking. What you desire is to rid yourself of Isfendiar."

Nevertheless he set out on this errand with a great army, and sent his eldest son before him with a message of friendship to the champion. Rustem, at the first, was indisposed to accept the Prince's friendship ; but

The Death of a Simorg.

listened when his father said, " Let us go and meet the Prince. Have we not always paid our duty to his house. Let us go and offer him such entertainment as becomes his birth."

Accordingly Rustem went to meet Isfendiar, and when he approached his camp, dismounted from his horse, and went on foot to pay him his respects. After the two had embraced, Rustem said, " I pray you to come to my house. We will entertain you according to the best of our power."

The Prince answered : " The King my father has forbidden me to enter any house in this country. But let me put the irons on your feet, and suffer me to take you bound to the King. You shall suffer no harm ; indeed the irons shall not remain till night. If you will consent to this, when the crown shall come to me, I will put the whole world under your power."

Rustem answered : " It would be a lasting shame to me if a Prince such as you are should refuse to come under my roof. As for the irons, I cannot suffer them ; but everything else that you command I will do."

The Prince said : "I cannot disobey the commands of the King my father by coming under your roof. But come and feast with me. Let us enjoy the present. Why need we think of the future ?"

So Rustem departed to put on such a dress as was suitable for a banquet. But when he was gone the Prince said to himself, "Why should I seek friendship with this man ? I will not invite him."

Rustem waited long for the invitation, and was grievously offended that it did not come. At last he said, "I will go and talk to this courteous Prince, and tell him my mind."

When he arrived at the Prince's tent, he said, "Young man, these are strange customs that you introduce. Was not, then, your guest worth so much as a message ?"

The Prince excused himself by saying, "The day was hot, and the way was long, and I was unwilling to trouble you. But now as you came, sit down by my side and drink a cup of wine with me."

So saying, he offered Rustem a place at his left hand. But Rustem said, "I have never sat but at the right hand of kings." So they gave him a place at the Prince's right hand.

The Prince then said: " I have heard that your father Zal, when he was born, was of so unsightly an appearance that his father could not bear to look on him; and that even the Simorg, when he was exposed on the mountain, would not carry him as food for her young."

Rustem answered: "Why do you use such injurious words ? " And he proceeded to describe the greatness of his family, and to enumerate his own achievements. And the Prince, on the other hand, boasted of his own race and of what he had himself accomplished.

When they had thus talked together for a time, Isfendiar said: "We have boasted enough. I am hungry and thirsty; let us eat and drink. To-morrow we will try each other's strength on the field of battle."

Isfendiar ordered meat and drink to be brought, and they sat down to table. All were astonished to see Rustem's appetite. Joint after joint of roasted lamb did he eat, till the Prince could scarcely believe his eyes.

At last he said: "Bring us wine; let it be new wine, not old. We will see how Rustem will behave himself when he has well drunk."

The cupbearer brought a goblet so great that no one could have believed it possible that a man could empty it; but Rustem drained every drop, drinking to the health of the King of Kings. The cupbearer brought it again full; but the hero said: "This wine wants no water; water does but spoil it."

So the Prince said: "Bring another cup without water."

But Rustem astonished him more and more.

When the time of departure was come, Rustem said: "Prince, I pray you to come under my roof, though it be but for a few hours. Listen to the voice of reason, and let us be at peace."

Isfendiar answered: "As for coming under your roof, I have spoken already. But listen to me. Suffer me to bind you and bring you before the King. Believe me that, if you will consent, he will think more highly of you than before."

"I cannot endure the disgrace of being

bound," said Rustem. "Did I suffer it, I should lose all the glory that I have gained. Why are you so bent on strife? Believe me, it will turn out ill both for your life and for mine."

The Prince answered: "Say no more; my purpose is fixed. To-morrow, on the field of battle, we will see who is the better man."

But when Rustem was departing, Isfendiar said to his brother: "I am astonished at this hero, so strong is he, so noble in countenance. Nevertheless the orders of the King must be obeyed, and to-morrow I will darken for him the light of the sun."

His brother answered: "Listen to me. Go to-morrow without escort to the hero's palace. I am sure that his heart is full of loyalty to the King and to you. Speak peaceably to him, and banish this unreasonable anger from your heart."

The Prince made no reply; he was bent on his own fall.

On the other hand, the old man Zal urgently entreated his son that he should not fight with the Prince. "If you fall," he said, "by the hand of this young man, the glory of our house is departed. If you kill him, you kill the son of a king, and you cover yourself with disgrace. Go and submit yourself to him; if you will not do that, ransom yourself with all your treasures. Whatever you do, do not fight with the Prince."

Rustem said: "I spoke peaceably to him, but he would not hear me. Nevertheless, have no fear for his life; I will not wound him. No; I will snatch him from his saddle and carry him off a prisoner. Then he shall be my guest; and when we are friends I will take and set him on the throne of Persia."

Zal smiled to hear such talk from his son.

" These are foolish words," he said. " Do you talk of carrying off the son of the King and bringing him to my palace? This is not such a thing as you should say."

And he bowed his head to the ground and prayed: " O Judge and Master of the World, deliver us from our troubles."

The next day, as soon as it was light, Rustem armed himself for battle, and went out to meet Isfendiar, who also armed himself, and leapt on the back of his charger, as a leopard leaps on to the back of a wild ass. So the two met together, the old warrior and the young.

But, first, Rustem again attempted to turn Isfendiar from his purpose.

"If you are bent," said he, "on battle, why not bid your Persians advance? I, on my part, will command my warriors of Zabulistan to charge. We can sit here in peace, and see others fight till we are satisfied."

"This is folly," answered Isfendiar; "what quarrel is there between Persia and Zabulistan? Let our armies remain in peace. We two will fight, and will see whether Isfendiar's charger will return riderless to his stable, or Raksh go back without his master to the palace of Zal."

Then the two champions delayed no longer, but fell upon each other. First they fought with their spears, and when these were broken they drew their swords, and when their swords were shivered to pieces they seized their clubs, and when the handles of the clubs were broken by the violence of their blows, they threw their lassos; each caught the other round the body; each used all his strength to drag his adversary from the saddle, but neither could prevail. So they fought till both they and their horses were worn-out with weariness.

In the meanwhile, the lieutenants of Rustem had provoked a battle between the two armies, and in this battle two valiant youths, sons of Prince Isfendiar, were killed. When Isfendiar heard this bad news he was transported with rage.

"Is this the way," he cried to Rustem, "that nobles keep treaties? Do you hear this, that your chiefs have killed my two sons?"

Rustem said: "I swear by the head of the King, and by the sun, and by my sword, that this is no doing of mine. Whoever has been in fault, though it were my own brother, I will bind him hand and foot and carry him before the King, and you shall have vengeance for the blood of your sons."

"It is idle," answered the Prince, "to kill the snake to avenge the peacock's death. No—save yourself, for your last hour has come."

Thus saying, he seized his bow and arrows, and rained a shower of arrows on Rustem and Raksh. Sixty arrows there were in all, and there was not one of them but what wounded the hero or his horse. But Rustem, with his arrows, did not inflict so much as a single wound upon his adversary. The hero felt all his strength passing from him, and said :

" It is enough for to-day ; night is at hand, and no one can fight in the darkness. Go to your tent, and I will return to my palace, and rest awhile, and heal my wounds. And I will call my best counsellors togethers, and we will consider whether we will not obey your commands."

Isfendiar said : " Old man, you know many stratagems and devices. Do not think that you deceive me. But go—I spare your life for to-night."

So Rustem departed. And Isfendiar went to his tent and lamented over the death of his two sons. Their bodies he sent to the King in coffins of gold on biers of ebony, with this message :

" See the firstfruits of your devices ! Isfendiar is yet alive, but I know not what fate is in store for him. He is consumed with sorrow, and you enjoy the pleasures of the throne ; but remember that these pleasures do not last for ever."

Meanwhile Rustem held council with Zal his father, and with the chiefs.

"I am in despair," he said. "Never before have I met a warrior who could resist me; but now I am helpless against this Isfendiar. My arrows could no more pierce his cuirass than a thorn can pierce a rock. If it had not been for the darkness, he had certainly slain me. Nothing remains for me but to mount on Raksh and ride away to some distant country where this terrible enemy shall not be able to find me."

Zal said : "My son, listen to me. There is yet one hope of safety. We will call the Simorg to our help."

Immediately Zal climbed a high mountain, taking with him three censers filled with fire, and being accompanied by three magicians. When he reached the crest of the mountain, he took out a feather which was wrapped in a piece of brocade, and stirring the fire in one of the censers, burnt the feather. At the end of the first watch, the night suddenly became darker than before : it was the Simorg, which had spied the glimmer of the fire. The bird approached in great circles, and Zal rose from the ground with the magicians, who all the while were burning incense, and did homage to it.

The Simorg said, " Prince, why have you called me by burning this feather?"

" Because my house is in danger," answered Zal. " Rustem is so grievously wounded that I fear for his life ; and Raksh, his horse, is nearly dead."

The Simorg said, " Let me see the warrior and his horse."

So Zal sent for Rustem and Raksh ; and they came, though they had scarcely strength to move.

The Simorg examined their wounds, and first drew from the hero's body four arrow-heads. Then he sucked the blood from the wounds with his beak ; lastly he rubbed them with his wings. Rustem, in a moment, felt all his strength return to him.

" Dress the wounds," said the Bird, " and take care for seven days not to hurt yourself. If you will dip one of my feathers in milk, and pass it over the places, they will soon be -healed."

Then he did the same service to Raksh, drawing from his body six arrow-heads. The horse's strength came back, and he neighed, to his master's great joy."

" Why," said the Simorg, " did you seek to do battle with Isfendiar ? "

" He would have chained me," answered Rustem, " and my soul could not endure such dishonour."

" Listen to me," said the Simorg again. " Offer your homage to this son of a king, Surrender yourself to him. If his hour is come, he will refuse your submission ; if that be so, I know a way of delivering you."

The Bird then led the way to a tamarisk-tree.

" Choose," said he to the hero, " the straightest, longest, and finest branch that you can find. To this branch is bound the fate of Isfendiar. Make it straight before the fire ; look out a well-tempered arrow-head for it ; feather it well ; and if it is Isfendiar's hour to die, this is the weapon by which he will perish."

Rustem did exactly as the Bird had commanded him. When the time was come, he presented himself before Isfendiar, and offered his submission. "Only," he said, "spare me the chains ; they will disgrace me for ever."

"This is idle talk," said the Prince ; "choose between chains and battle."

Then Rustem, seeing that his submission was not accepted, bent his bow, and laid the arrow of tamarisk-wood in rest, and so held it, while he prayed in secret to God. The Prince, seeing him delay, thought that he did it from fear, and taunted him. Then Rustem hesitated no longer, but let the arrow fly, aiming at the Prince's eye. The arrow flew straight at its mark, and Isfendiar's strength left him in a moment ; his bow dropped from his hand, and he seized his horse's mane.

"You have reaped as you have sown," cried Rustem ; "you thought yourself an invincible hero, and now a single arrow has robbed you of all your strength."

As he spoke, the Prince dropped from his horse upon the ground. There he lay sense- less for a while ; then, sitting up on the ground, he drew the arrow from his eye, covered as it was with blood from the steel to the feathers.

Two of his nobles, seeing what had happened, ran up and lifted him from the ground, uttering loud cries of grief and despair. The white-haired Zal also hastened to the place, and lamented over this misfortune.

" The wise men have told me," he cried, "that the man who slays Isfendiar, will have no peace either in this world or in the next."

Isfendiar said : " Trouble not yourselves. It is not Rustem that has slain me, nor the Simorg, nor the magical arrow. It is my father who sent me to my death. But do you, Rustem, take my son Bahman in your charge ; teach him the ways of a king, for it has been foretold to me that he will sit upon the throne that has been denied to me."

Rustem laid his right hand upon his heart, and swore that he would do as Isfendiar had said.

Then the soul of Isfendiar was satisfied.

This was the last victory of Rustem.

CHAPTER XIII.

THE DEATH OF RUSTEM.

ZAL of the white hair had born to him in his old age a son of singular beauty. But when the astrologers came to cast his horoscope, they were perplexed and terrified at what they found. They said to Zal, "We have learnt the secret of the heavens; but it is of evil import for you and yours. This beautiful son will be the ruin of your house; he will confound the land of Persia; few and bitter will be his own days, and there will be few of his kindred that will survive him."

Zal gave the lad the name of Sheghad, and sent him, when he was grown up, to the King of Cabul. When the King saw that he was tall and handsome, and fit in all respects to sit upon a throne, he showed him great kindness, provided for him bountifully, and finally gave him his daughter in marriage.

Rustem was accustomed to receive every year from the King of Cabul a bull's hide, as a token of sovereignty; and the King hoped that, now that Sheghad was become his son-in-law, this tribute would be remitted. But when the proper time came, Rustem sent his messenger as usual, and demanded the bull's hide.

The King, and still more Sheghad, were greatly offended at this conduct.

"Why should I respect my elder brother," said he, "when he is not ashamed to behave to me so unkindly? I care for him no more than if he were a stranger."

One night the King and his son-in-law could not sleep for thinking of this affair, but sat talking of how they might rid the world of Rustem. At last Sheghad said to the King:

" Listen to my scheme. Make a great feast, and invite all the nobles to it; while we are drinking wine, say something insulting to me. I will leave the table, as if in anger, and, going to Zabulistan, will complain to my father and my brother of the King of Cabul. Then Rustem will come to redress my wrongs. You must find a hunting-ground, and cause a number of pits to be dug in it; they must be dug large enough for Rustem and Raksh, his horse. The bottom of the pits must be filled with swords and lances and hunting spears, with their handles in the earth and their points upwards. Let a great number of them be dug, a hundred rather than five; and take care that you say nothing of the matter—no, not even to the sun."

So the King made a feast, and invited to it all the nobles of the land. When their heads were full of the fumes of wine, Sheghad began to boast of his parentage.

"There is no one equal to me in this company," he cried. "Zal is my father, and Rustem my brother."

The King said: "You are no brother of Rustem. You are the son of a slave!"

Then Sheghad started up in a rage, and left the banqueting hall, and set out for Zabulistan. When he came to the palace, his brother asked him: "How do you fare in Cabul?"

Sheghad said: "Do not speak to me of

Cabul. The King has insulted me beyond bearing; yes, and you too. 'You are no son of Zal,' he said, 'and, though you were, it would be nothing to your honour.' Then I came away in a rage."

Rustem said : " My brother, do not trouble yourself about this fellow. I will humble him in the dust, and give his crown to you."

Then Rustem commanded his lieutenants to assemble an army; but Sheghad said : " Do not trouble yourself to lead an army against Cabul. The mere sound of your name will be enough. Already, I am sure, the King repents of his folly, and he will send his chiefs to entreat your pardon."

" You are right," said Rustem, " I have no need to take an army against Cabul. A hundred horsemen will be sufficient."

Meanwhile the King of Cabul had caused the pits to be made according to Sheghad's advice. They were so skilfully hidden, that neither man nor horse could possibly discover them.

As soon as Rustem had set out, Sheghad sent a message to the King. " Rustem has set

The Chase

out without an army. Come and make a pretence of entreating his pardon."

So the King came to meet Rustem, his tongue covered with honey, his heart full of poison. And as soon as he spied him in the distance, he dismounted, uncovered his head, drew his shoes from his feet, and, throwing himself on the ground, begged pardon for the injurious words that he had used to Sheghad. So Rustem pardoned him, and accompanied him on his return to his capital.

Near the city the King had had a feast prepared in a beautiful garden ; and, as they sat at the wine, he said : " If you have any wish to hunt, I have a park where the plains and hills abound with wild beasts. There are lions among the hills, and in the plain roe-deer and wild asses."

Rustem heard this with delight, for his fate had come upon him. He bade Raksh be saddled, took his falcons, and put his bow in its case, and set out. As they were following the chase, all his companions left him, and he—for so fate would have it—approached the place where the pits had been dug. Raksh, however, smelt the newly-turned earth, and reared, and would not advance. But Rustem was d etermined to go on,and, blinded by his fate, lifted his whip in a rage, and touched Raksh, though but lightly, with it. The horse bounded at the stroke, and fell with two of his feet in one of the pits. His sides were terribly wounded, and Rustem's breast and legs were also pierced. Nevertheless, such **was** his strength, he disentangled himself from the trap, and recovered his footing on the side of the pit.

When he opened his eyes he saw Sheghad, and knew from his face that he had contrived this treachery. "You will repent of this," he cried.

But Sheghad said : "You have deserved your end for all the blood that you have shed."

At this moment the King arrived, and when he saw how seriously Rustem was wounded, he pretended to be grieved, and said : "How has this misfortune happened ? I will go at once and fetch physicians to heal your wounds."

"The time is past," answered Rustem, "when physicians can help me. I am passing away, as better men before me have passed.

The Death of Rustum

But be sure that my son will avenge my death."

Then he turned to Sheghad and said: "Grant me this one favour. Give me my bow and two arrows. I would not be torn in pieces by a lion, as I lie helpless here."

Sheghad drew the bow from its case, and put it into Rustem's hand, smiling, as he did so, with joy that his brother was dying. Rustem griped it with a mighty grasp, weakened though he was with the pain of his wounds. When Sheghad saw how strong he was, he was struck with terror, and tried to hide himself. There was a plane-tree close at hand, and behind this he sheltered himself. But Rustem laid an arrow in rest, and drew his bow with such strength that the arrow passed right through both the tree and Sheghad. The hero rejoiced and said: "Thanks be to God that I have been able to revenge myself on this traitor." And as he spoke his spirit left him.

This was the end of Rustem.

THE STORY OF KEHAMA.

18

THE STORY OF KEHAMA.

CHAPTER I.

THE CURSE.

It was midnight in Kehama's city, and yet there was not a man, or woman, or child, that slept from one end of it to the other ; it was midnight, and yet the streets were bright as at noonday. For Kehama, the great Rajah, made a splendid funeral for his dead son. First in the procession came the priests, the Brahmins, and after them the dead man, seated upright in his palankeen. There is a glow on his cheek, but it is only from the curtains of crimson silk ; he nods his heads, but it is only from the motion of the bearers' steps. Close behind his son came the great Rajah himself, and next to him, each in her gilded palankeen, the dead man's wives, who are doomed to die with their lord; and after these again, closely guarded by a company of bowmen, a man and a girl. The man is Ladurlad; it was he who dealt Arvalan his death-blow; the girl is Kailyal, his daughter; it was in defending her that Ladurlad did the deed.

And now the funeral rites are finished; nothing but ashes remains of the dead man's body; and Kehama, approaching the great slab of stone on which it had been laid for the burning, spreads on it honey and rice, and calls on the spirit of his son. The spirit comes, though none but Kehama could perceive the thin unsubstantial form. " Is this all that you can do for me," said Arvalan, "this funeral pomp and show, you who are mightier than the gods ? "

Kehama's grief was changed to anger at this reproach. " Fool," he cried, " fool that you were, when I had secured you against fire, and sword, and the common accidents of man, to perish by a stake in a peasant's hand! In a little time I could have made you safe against death itself."

"It is useless to reproach me," answered Arvalan; "it was my hour of folly, and my fate was too strong for me. But is there nothing that you can do for me? The elements, fire and air and water, torture my naked soul."

"They shall do so no more," said Kehama. "Is there anything else that you desire."

"Yes," cried the spirit, "vengeance!"

Then Kehama turned, and raising his hand to silence the crowd, said : "Bring forth the murderer."

Ladurlad stepped forward at the word, but Kailyal hung back, looking round for help, though indeed she knew that help there was none. Now it so chanced that on the brink of the river was a wooden image, roughly carved, of Marriataly, the goddess of the poor. When Kailyal saw it, she sprang to it, and clasped it tightly with her arms. The guards seized her, and would have dragged her away ; but as they dragged she clung still closer and closer. And now, as the image rocks and bends with the strain, they fancy that the girl is slackening her hold, and drag with redoubled effort, when, of a sudden, the image yields to their force ; and as it yields, the bank crumbles, and gives way under their feet, and all, the guards and the girl alike, are plunged headlong into the stream.

"She has escaped me," said the Rajah, "but the more guilty criminal is left." And he looked with a dreadful frown at Ladurlad.

"Mercy!" cried the wretched man, "mercy! It was only to save my child that I slew the Prince. Mercy!"

Kehama said not a word, but stood buried in meditation. He had no thought of mercy; he made no account of right and justice; he considered only how his vengeance might be most complete. At last he spoke.

"Ladurlad," he said, "I charm thy life from steel and stone and wood, from the bite of the serpent, from the tooth of the wild beast, from sickness, and from time. Earth is mine, and it shall deny thee its fruits; water is mine, and it shall fly from thy approach; the winds are mine, and they shall pass by thee. Thou shalt seek death, but shalt seek it in vain. Thou shalt live with an unquenched fire in thy heart and thy brain as long as my power shall last."

And he turned away to the crowd; and Ladurlad wandered away, overwhelmed with his misery. His feet took him, not knowing or caring whither he went, to the river bank; and there he spied something floating down the stream. It seemed like the trunk of a tree; but as he was turning away, he caught a glimpse of a woman's robe. "Ah!" he thought to himself, "the goddess has saved her," and he plunged into the river. The water knew the spell that Kehama had laid upon it, and shrunk before him, and almost in a moment he had caught his daughter in his arms, and drawn her to the shore. There he laid her on the sand, and chafed her heart and her feet, laying them bare to the warmth of the sun. Long he laboured with scarcely a hope; at last her eyelids began to tremble, and then her lips, and after her bosom to heave. She lived again.

When she opened her eyes, and saw her father, a thrill of hope shot through her. "He has spared us, then," she cried.

He shook his head. "He has laid a curse upon me, a curse which will cling to me for ever. No wind may breathe on me; no water touch me. Sleep may never light on me; and even death itself is denied to me."

The girl looked at him incredulously; but when she put her hand on his garments, and found them still dry, though he had brought her from the depths of the river, she knew that he had spoken the truth.

CHAPTER II.

THE GLENDOVEER.

ALL that day the unhappy Ladurlad and his daughter wandered across the plain and through the jungle. They had no care or thought of the way, except, indeed, to be as far as possible from Kehama's city. When darkness overtook them they were at a place where a white flag marked the spot where some poor victim had been seized by a tiger. At other times they would have fled from the neighbourhood as from a pestilence. Now Ladurlad was beyond all fear, as he was beyond all hope, and Kailyal had no thought except for her father. There, then, they lay down to rest, though there was no rest for the unhappy Ladurlad. Still, for his daughter's sake, he feigned to be asleep, and she, listening to his regular breathing, and hoping against hope, began to believe that the gods might have had pity upon him, and given him a respite from the pain of the curse. So she sat and listened, till at last, wearied as she was with her day's wandering, sleep overtook her, and she ceased her watch.

Then Ladurlad thought to himself: "Why should I cumber this innocent girl with my unhappy company ? Why should she bear the burden of a woe which she cannot relieve?" He lifted his head from her lap. She did not wake. He stood up, and still she slept. Silently he stole away ; then she felt that he was gone. For a moment she stood, listening to his steps and not knowing what to do. Then, with a shriek, she rushed after him ; but the night and the thickness of the jungle hindered her, and he quickened his steps when he was aware of her pursuit.

While she stood utterly perplexed, she heard the howl of a tiger in the distance. But when she turned, something more dreadful encountered her—a human form, a shape of lurid light, dimly seen in the darkness. Nearer and nearer

Kaitval.

it came, as she stood spell-bound with horror; and she knew the face of Arvalan! The spectre stretched out its hands to clasp her. Then the spell was broken, and she fled. It so chanced that by the wayside was a temple, the temple of Pollear, the elephant-headed god to whom travellers pray, standing with doors wide open. The maiden rushed headlong into the shrine, and clasped the altar. Even at the altar the pursuing spectre seized her. But the insulted god caught him with his elephant-trunk, and hurled him, as a stone is hurled by a catapult, into the depths of the forest.

Kailyal did not stay to see how she had been saved, but, rushing on wildly through the jungle, struck her foot on the root of a man chineel-tree, and there lay, like one dead, under the poisonous shade.

It so chanced that one of the Glendoveers, the winged children of Casyapa, the Father of the gods, was abroad that night, disporting himself in the air. He chanced to see Kailyal as she lay, and pitying one so beautiful and so unhappy, bore her to his father's abode.

Said Casyapa to his son—Ereenia was the name of the Glendoveer : " Do you know what you have done, bringing a mortal into this holy place ? "

" I found her," said Ereenia, " under the shade of a poison-tree, lying lifeless as you see her."

" But what if she is a sinful mortal, one doomed to death ? "

" Sinful, my father! surely she cannot be with that sweet, innocent face. But, my father, why do you ask questions of me, you who know all things ? "

" Do you know Kehama ? "

" The Almighty Man ! Who does not know him and his fearful power ? Who does not know the tyrant of earth, and the enemy of heaven ? "

" Do you fear him ? "

" I know that he is terrible."

" Terrible indeed ! He has such power that there is hope even in hell; yes, and fear in heaven. The spirits of the condemned are glad ; the souls of the blessed suspend their joy. Nay, the very gods are afraid. Brahma

Glendoveers.

fears, and Veshnoo turns his face in doubt to Seeva's throne."

"I have seen Indra tremble at his prayers and dreadful penances, prayers and penances which claim from Seeva a power so vast that even he cannot grant it and be safe."

"Ereenia, will you dare this Almighty Man?"

"I, my father? I dare him?"

"If not, take the maid again to earth; drop her before the tiger, as he prowls for his prey, or under the poison-tree, that they may work Kehama's will."

"Never—never will I do it."

"Then meet his wrath."

"But why not shelter her here, my father?"

"My son, it cannot be. I have piety and wisdom and peace; but I have not the strength to resist this almighty Kehama, no, nor even the spirit of the dead Arvalan."

"Arvalan!"

"Kehama has given his dead son all the faculties of which the dead are capable, until his hour of judgment comes."

"See! she lives! And lo! her hand touches the Holy River at its sources. Were there anything impure in that hand, the waters would shrink from it. But see, they play about it, and leap, and sparkle, as if to welcome her."

"Of a truth she is pure from sin," cried Casyapa. "But, my son, what will you do with the maid?" for now, at the bidding of the Glendoveer, a ship of heaven came sailing down the skies.

"My father," answered Ereenia, "I will carry her straight to the Swerga, to Indra's own dwelling. Indra is the foe of her foe, and he should protect her. But if the god shrinks from the Rajah's might, and is unwilling to try the perilous ship, then, small as I am, I will stand forth and plead the maiden's cause in the presence of Seeva himself."

"It is well," said the Father of the gods; "it is well. Stand forth without fear; and whatever may befall, still trust in Him. He will do and cause to be done that which is right."

The ship of heaven went on its way and carried the Glendoveer and the maiden on their way to the Paradise of Swerga, the dwelling of

Indra. When they had reached it, he said to her: "Rest in peace, maiden. Feeble as I am, I will guard you. The Almighty Rajah shall not harm you, so long as Indra keeps his throne."

"Ah," cried Kailyal, "and you too fear him!"

"So long as the Swerga is safe, you are safe also."

"But save not me only. I have a most unhappy father; Kehama's curse is on him. Can you not save him also?"

"Come, plead your cause to Indra himself."

So saying, he lifted Kailyal on his wings, and carried her to where Indra sat upon his throne.

There was trouble on the face of the god, and it grew darker and deeper when he saw Ereenia and the mortal maid.

Ereenia said: "Hear me, Indra. I found this child of man brought near to death, I know not by what mishap. I carried her to the dwelling of the Father of the gods, intending, when she should have been healed, to restore her to earth. But when I heard her fate, I had other thoughts. She is one of those who groan beneath the power of the Almighty Rajah, and she is persecuted by the spectre of his dead son Arvalan. What choice had I but to bring her hither? Here she is safe, for here thou art yet supreme."

"Ereenia," answered the god, "no child of man may dwell in these bowers of bliss. With man must come Time and Wrath and Change; and these once come, our happiness would pass. A stronger hand than mine may wrest this Paradise from me; but I will do nothing to provoke the fate."

"Fear," said Ereenia, "courts the blow. Fear will lay us prostrate under the wheels of destiny."

"It may be," answered Indra, "that Veshnoo will again descend and serve the gods. Did he not save them before from another such Almighty Man, from Ravanen, killing him with the arrows that never fail?"

"It is an idle hope," said the Glendoveer. "Put forth thy own strength for thine own salvation. Would that the lightnings which play harmlessly about thy head were mine.

The overthrow of Ravanen.

The Swerga would not want a champion nor Earth a deliverer."

"Think you," cried Indra in wrath, "that I want the will to strike my enemy? But of a truth I can no more cast down this Kehama than can you. He went on from conquest to conquest till a'l the kings of the earth had received his yoke. When the steam of the sacrifice went up which was to proclaim him Omnipotent below, then was the time to strike him with the thunderbolt. That time went by; and now by prayers and penances he has wrested such power from Fate, that if Seeva turn not his eyes on earth and Veshnoo descend not to save, he will seize the Swerga for his own, and roll his chariot-wheels through Padalon, the dwelling of the dead, and force from Yamen's charge the cup of Immortality. My thunders cannot pierce the sphere of power which encompasses him."

"Take me to earth, blessed Spirit," cried Kailyal, when she heard the word of fate from Indra's mouth. "If my father must still bear the curse, he shall not bear it alone."

"Child of earth," said Indra, "thou hast

already the divine spirit, for duty is thy guide." Then he turned to Ereenia and said : " Take her to where the Ganges has his second birth. There may she and her father rest secure till the hour of doom shall come."

CHAPTER III.

LADURLAD.

FOR ninety-and-nine days, day after day,
Kehama had led the victim, a horse which
no man had bestridden, to Seeva's shrine.
One more day, one more victim, and the rite
will be complete; Kehama will then have
accomplished his desire; the power of Heaven
as of Earth will be his, and he will seize the
throne and wield the thunderbolts of Indra.
Is Seeva the Destroyer blind? Why does
not Veshnoo descend to save mankind and
the gods?

For a year and a day the steed destined
for the sacrifice has wandered where he would.
No man's hand has combed his mane; his
mouth has never felt bit or bridle; to-day at
noon he must bleed; and then Kehama grasps

against the very will of Fate, the power which he desires.

It is high noon, and the many guards which, lest anything by chance should mar the sacrifice, have kept the victim in sight, contracts its circle, and drives him in towards the shrine. In long files before the temple court stand the Rajah's archers; between them, starting and flinging up his head, moves on the untamed steed, and the multitude closes up the rear; while in front the white-robed Brahmins stand with the axe prepared with which Kehama is to complete the sacrifice.

Within the temple, on his golden couch, with the attendants fanning him with peacock plumes, lies the great Rajah, watching the perfumed light that measures out the hours as they pass. And now the time is come; the sun is at its height in the heavens; he rises from his couch and takes the axe in his hand, ready to strike the victim.

That instant with a loud cry sprang a man from out the crowd. A thousand archers loosed their bows, as they stood with their arrows at rest; not a shaft missed its aim.

Kehama.

But it was in vain that they fell upon him, thick as a storm of hail. Kehama clasped his hands in agony as he saw the daring wretch grasp the horse's mane, spring with a sudden bound upon its back, and gallop furiously round and round.

They seized him; they dragged him to the Rajah's feet. What tortures are in store for him? What new punishment will the baffled tyrant invent? The multitude, standing silent, but with hatred and curses in their hearts, tremble to think. But the man himself is calm as death. There was even a ghastly smile upon his lips, and a dreadful hope in his eye. "Yes, Rajah," he cried, "it is I! Wilt thou kill me now?"

Kehama's face fell when he saw Ladurlad. "That wretch again!" he cried; and he struck his forehead, and stood awhile in silent rage. Then with a bitter smile he said: "Let him go; he has the curse; he can suffer nothing more. But ye," and he turned in fury to the archers, "ye who did not stop him, tremble ye."

Then he commanded the archers to pile their arms, and calling his horsemen, bade them hem in the offenders, and slay till not a man was left alive.

Once more 'Ladurlad, left to go whither he would, wandered away; and this time his feet carried him unwittingly to his own home. He found it deserted and desolate. As he sat and thought of his unhappy lot, and the child whom he had left and lost, he heard a sound of mocking laughter that seemed to come from the air, and looking up he saw the face of the dead Arvalan. Only the face it was, without a body, and the eyes shone with a lurid light as of sulphur. Well Ladurlad knew that hateful countenance, and seizing from the ground a blackened stake—it was the very stake with which he had slain him, and the dead man's blood was still upon it—he tried once and again to strike the spectre. Again the face laughed in scorn; then there seemed to come forth a hand, which caught the sunbeams, and turned its heat and light condensed upon Ladurlad. It was a useless cruelty! The stake fell from his hand, burned to white ashes, but the man felt no new pain. Kehama's curse had charmed 'him from such suffering,

Kehama's Archers sh.... .... Ladurlad.

so fierce was the fire already in his heart and brain.

Then the spectre put out another hand, and a whirlwind came down from the sky, and scooping up the sand like smoke, sent down the burning shower upon Ladurlad's head. Whichever way he turned, the accursed hand waved to guide the burning storm.

But help was at hand. Ereenia, his heavenly sword in hand, hastened down from the height. Thrice he drove it through the spectre, till the foul creature fled, howling with pain. Then he called the ship of heaven. Obedient to his word it came, and Kailyal in it ; and there by the daughter's side he laid the father, still dizzy with the storm of burning sand.

Swift through the air the ship bore that happy company, Ladurlad, and Kailyal, and the Glendoveer, and carried them to the place where the persecuted father and child were to rest till the struggle between Kehama and the gods should be finished. There was some time of respite, for the final sacrifice had to be begun again from the beginning ; and till this should be done, earth and heaven alike had peace.

One evening during this happy period the Glendoveer was displaying to Kailyal, as she sat by the spring of the holy river, his power of flight, spreading his dark-blue wings, and now gliding over the surface of the lake, now rising into the air, now diving into the depths of the water. Camdeo, the boy-god of Love, came by, riding on his parrot, having in his hand the bow of sugar-cane, the string of which is made of flowers, and the arrows are tipped with poison. He aimed a shaft at the Glendoveer, and struck him full on the breast, but the arrow dropped without harming him.

"Go!" cried the Glendoveer, "aim at idler hearts. My love for the maid is deeper than comes from thy arrows."

Meanwhile the god had aimed a second arrow at Kailyal; but before he could let it fly, the string broke in his hand.

"See!" cried the Glendoveer, again, "thou hast no power for mischief here."

So the days of rest passed by.

Camdeo.

CHAPTER IV.

THE time came—all too soon—when Kehama's sacrifice was duly completed, and the Almighty Rajah became Lord of the Paradise of Swerga. Casyapa and the other gods retreated to the second sphere, and Ladurlad and his daughter were compelled to return to the earth. For some time they lived unmolested, choosing for their home an ancient banyan-tree, whose fifty trunks, self-planted in the ground, made a welcome shade both from sun and storm. At last some ill-chance brought to the place a band of the devotees of Juggernaut, who, seeing the wonderful beauty of Kailyal, seized her, and carried her off to be the bride of their god.

There, in the temple, on the feast day when the great car is dragged by the frantic crowds,

Arvalan, who had summoned to his aid a powerful sorceress named Lorrinite, would have seized her. The Glendoveer, indeed, hearing her cry for help, appeared on the instant, and catching the foul creature raised him to the temple, and dashed him howling to the floor. But when the earth was in Kehama's power, it was not the time for good spirits to prevail, and Lorrinite summoned a host of demons to her help, and commanded them to seize and bind him. In vain did he ply his sword of heavenly temper; their numbers overpowered him, and now there were no gods to help.

"Carry him," cried Lorrinite the sorceress, "to the ancient tombs beneath the sea. The gods cannot help him now, and for man there is no way thither."

So the demons carried the Glendoveer away to the tombs.

Meanwhile the sorceress restored the shattered form of Arvalan. But when he turned again to seize the maiden Kailyal, she in her despair caught up a torch, and set fire to the hangings of the temple. In a moment the whole shrine was wrapped in flames. Confounded with the blaze, Lorrinite and Arvalan fled from the place ; but, when Kailyal was about to throw herself into the fire, Ladurlad, plunging unharmed through the flames, caught her in his arms, and carried her safely away. And so again the power of the curse preserved the innocent, whom it had been intended to destroy.

" Ereenia !" cried Kailyal, when she began to breathe again.

" My child," said Ladurlad, " do not reproach him. Evil now rules the world, and no good spirit can venture here."

" Nay," answered Kailyal, " but he did venture, and the demons beat him down, and carried him off to the tombs beneath the sea. So said their hideous mistress, and she boasted that there are now no gods to help, and that there is no way for man to that place."

" See again," said Ladurlad, " how short-sighted is wickedness ! Truly there is no way for man to the tombs beneath the sea, for the waves surround and cover them ; but I am not as other men."

" Let us go," cried Kailyal, " to set him free."

For many days they journeyed, and as they went Ladurlad told his daughter the story of Baly, the great Rajah—how he had conquered the earth and seized the heavens; and how he fell. The story was this :—

When the conqueror had seated himself on the throne of the Swerga, Veshnoo came and stood before him in the shape of a dwarfish Brahmin. "Give me, great Rajah," said the god, "three steps, and no more, of thy great kingdom;" and Baly, who never refused a suppliant's prayer, answered : "Take thy boon, and measure it where thou wilt." Then Veshnoo with one step measured the earth, and with a second measured the heavens. "Where shall I take the third?" said the god; and the Rajah knew him, and prostrating himself before him, begged for pardon. And pardon was granted him. He was cast down indeed to Padalon, the abode of the dead; but, because he had always loved the right, and done justice, he was permitted to sit at the steps of the throne of Yamen—Yamen who is the Lord of Padalon— and there to judge the dead; and it was also granted him that once in the year he should

ascend to the upper air, and hear his name still
honoured by mankind, and rejoice in the fame
of his good deeds.

At last they came in their journey to where
the towers of Baly's city rose up in the sea.
Still splendid with gold, they shone out of the
dark-blue waves; but the city itself was covered
with the waters.

"Wait here for me," said Ladurlad; "this is
a vast region which I must explore, and my
search cannot be finished in one or two days.
These caverns in the rock will shelter you, and
the sea will cast up day by day food for you to
eat."

The sea closed above Ladurlad's head and
arched him over, as he walked with steady step
down the sloping shore, till he came to the
gates of the ancient city. Wide open they
stood, as they had been left on the day when
the people had fled from the rising sea. Through
solitary streets and squares he made his way,
till he came to the palace itself, in which the
great Rajah had held his court. Before the
palace door stood a great image, with crown
and sceptre laid at its feet, and in one hand

a scroll, to which the other hand pointed. On this scroll were written these words : *My name is Death; in mercy the Gods appointed me.* Beneath the image were two brazen gates wide open, and between the gates a staircase hewn in the living stone, which led to the ancient tombs. This hall of death was a low-roofed chamber, wide and long; and on either side, each in his own alcove, each on his own throne, each holding his sceptre, sat the kings of old. So well had the embalmers done their work, that every corpse had still the look of life ; but the royal robes with which they had been once arrayed had mouldered into nothingness, and they sat naked upon their thrones, statues of actual flesh, staring before them with fixed and meaningless eyes.

At the further end of the chamber, in the place where the great Rajah himself would have sat, had he not been exempted from the common lot of men, Ereenia lay, bound with strong fetters to the rock. Before him lay crouched a monster of the deep which the sorcerers had set there to keep guard over him; a hideous shape, of which the upper part was human, only that the skin was compact with scale on scale, and that the mouth, reaching from ear to ear, showed a triple row of teeth, with tusks on either side. The lower part was a double snake, winding in heavy coils.

With red and kindling eye the monster saw a living man approach, and rose in fury with half-open mouth to seize its prey. Then springing forward, flung its scaly arms about Ladurlad's heels, and sought to suck the life-blood from his veins. And, indeed, but for the curse the creature would have rent him to pieces as easily as a child crops a flower in the meadows; but again the evil was turned to good, and the man stood fearless and unharmed.

Then Ladurlad addressed himself to the conflict, and seized with both hands the monster's throat. In vain he pressed with a throttling grasp those impenetrable scales; and in vain, on the other hand, the beast wreathed round his adversary his snaky folds. The tiger's strength, the mail of the rhinoceros, had availed nothing against that strength; but the man, protected by the curse, felt nothing.

Meanwhile the Glendoveer, raising himself from his bed of stone, strove again with desperate effort to pluck away his fetters. It was in vain—even his heavenly sinews failed in the effort, so mightily had the chain been strengthened by Lorrinite's deadly arts.

For six days and six nights the monster and the man struggled together; but on the seventh, worn out by this strange struggle with a strength that had been charmed against all weariness, the Guardian of the Tombs began to give way. Sleep and fatigue over-powered him; at last he sought to fly, but Ladurlad followed him with unceasing hostility till he lay at last lifeless underneath his feet.

" The work is done ! " he cried, " but another labour yet remains." And he eyed the fetters that bound the Glendoveer. Then, looking round, he spied in a seat above, the scymitar wielded of old by the King whose lifeless form there sat enthroned. The brightness of its blade was dim with time; but the spells with which it had been welded had not lost their power, and its temper was as keen as ever. Once again he struck, but to little purpose, for the water deadened the descending blow. Then Ladurlad dealt a further stroke—the baser metal yielded to the blow, and the Glendoveer stood again free.

In the meanwhile Kailyal had waited for her father; six days and nights she waited, and her hopes grew fainter and fainter as he delayed his return. The night of the seventh day chanced to be that on which, year by year, Baly, the judge of the dead, walks forth on earth to hear his praises from the lips of men. And as he wandered on his way, he saw the maiden stand weeping by the shore and looking anxiously over the sea. He was about to issue forth from his invisibility to find out the cause of her trouble, when he espied in the air beside her the two evil powers that were in alliance to harm her, the witch Lorrinite and Arvalan. He spied them, but him they could not see, as they watched their prey.

And now she saw floating towards the shore the lifeless form of the monster which Ladurlad had destroyed. The waves left their hideous burden at her feet, and when she saw that it was indeed dead, she was assured that her father was indeed victorious.

"Come, my father; come, Ereenia," she cried, and stretched out her hands to the sea ; and as she spoke the two rose from the deep, and the daughter threw herself into her father's arms. But as she turned from him to greet the Glendoveer, the hideous form of Arvalan burst upon her sight, and with Arvalan was Lorrinite and a host of the demons which attended her. Vain was all resistance; they seized Ladurlad and Ereenia and the maiden, when the voice which all the guilty dread was heard through the air : " Hold your accursed hands," it cried ; and the same instant Baly was seen putting forth on every side his hundred arms. The sorceress and her ministers and the dead Arvalan he seized. He did not tarry for an instant to meet the Almighty Rajah, but stamped his feet upon the earth, which opened wide and gave him way to his own judgment-seat.

Kehama saw it from the height of the Swerga, and came flying down swift as a thunderbolt. Fiercely he smote the ground, and cleft it asunder, and hurled his fiery spear into the abyss. He hurled it, but it came back to him, driven with equal force; and with it came a voice: "Not yet, O Rajah, hast thou won the realm of death. The earth and the heaven are thine; but so long as Yamen holds the throne of hell, thy son shall lie in torments there."

"Let him lie," cried the Rajah, "but, Yamen, hear me; prepare the cup of immortality against the day when I shall put my feet upon thy neck."

Then he turned to Ladurlad.

"Ladurlad," he said, "you and I have done alike the work of fate, not knowing what we did. But now that my power over heaven and earth is established, our enmity is ended. I take away the curse."

And at the instant the fire departed from Ladurlad's heart and brain.

"Maiden," cried the Rajah, turning to Kailyal, "fairer and better and destined to higher things than all the daughters of earth, listen to me. Fate has chosen thee to be Kehama's bride. I see that decree written on your forehead. You and I, alone of all human kind, are destined to drink the Amreeta cup of immortality. Come, then, ascend my throne, and share my kingdom with me."

"It cannot be," cried Kailyal; "my heart and conscience rebel against such a lot, whether fate will it or no."

Kehama's brow grew dark with anger. Still, suppressing his wrath, he said to Ladurlad: "Counsel your daughter; bid her bow to the kindly decrees of fate; and tell her that the curse must burn till she obeys."

"Rajah," said the dauntless man, "she needs no counsel of mine. And now listen to me. Though all else in heaven and earth bow to thee, yet man's will is free. So the gods ordered it for man, and so it is. Do your worst!"

"Obstinate fools!" cried Kehama, in his rage; "in vain do you resist my will and the will of fate. But till we meet again, suffer your deserts."

And he cursed them, and vanished through the sky.

CHAPTER V.

EVEN as the Rajah departed, Ladurlad felt the curse return with double force. This he could have borne in silence, but he groaned with pain when, looking at his child, he saw her beauty all disfigured and marred with leprosy. But Kailyal's heart never failed her for a moment.

"Ha, Rajah!" she cried, with a disdainful smile, "wise and wicked as thou art, thy vengeance is blind, and acts a friendly part. This deformity is better than thy suit; nay, safe in this, I can walk fearless through the world."

And as she spoke she lifted her face proudly to the heavens. But then she turned it again to the earth, and there was a tear in her eye —the tears of a woman's regret for her lost beauty; and for a moment, it may be, she thought in her heart, "This is a loathsome sight to man; will it be so also to him, to Ereenia, the immortal?" "Not so," she said to herself again; "the powers above behold the soul itself through the wrappings of mortality, and see that it is beautiful, so long as it is free from sin."

But where is the Glendoveer?

He is gone in search of Seeva's throne, to tell before the very seat of supreme power his tale of wrong. How shall he find it? Do not the wise men say that when Brahma and Veshnoo contended for the pre-eminence, Seeva ended their strife, standing before them in his might like a mighty column of which they could not see the height or depth; that for a thousand years Veshnoo explored the depth, and Brahma for as long sought to reach the height, and neither found an end; and that, trembling and adoring, the rivals owned their lord? How shall the Glendoveer accomplish that which Brahma and Veshnoo failed to do? How shall he pass the seven worlds that, each with its own ocean, compass the mighty throne?

How shall he pierce the golden firmament that closes all within itself? Yet, he has done it; faith has given him power; space and time are as nothing to him. He journeys on till Seeva's seat appears, till he comes to Mount Calasay.

Seven ladders of silver stood around the mountain. So high they were that no one could see their top, and that worlds would decay with age before any one could climb from ring to ring; but the Glendoveer, his wings nerved with the strong power of faith, has climbed the highest, and reached the plain, the sanctuary above.

Then he lifted up his voice and spoke.

"There is oppression in the world below; earth groans beneath the yoke, and asks whether the avenger's eye is blinded that it cannot see. Holy One, awake! for mercy's sake put on thy terror, and, in justice to mankind, strike the blow!"

As he prayed thus, he felt his faith grow stronger and stronger in his heart. Then he spoke again—

"Let me not seek in vain, great Seeva! Thou art not here—for how should this con-

tain thee ?   Thou art not here—for how could
I endure thy presence ?   But thou art every-
where, and they who seek shall find."

When he had finished his prayer he sprang
up, and struck the great silver bell which hung
self-suspended above the plain.   It gave forth
in answer a deep melodious sound, and in a
moment Mount Calasay and the table and the
bell itself vanished away like a dream.   But
as he fell through space, the Glendoveer heard
a voice from within, which said—

"Go, ye who suffer, go to the throne of
Yamen ; he hath a remedy for every sorrow ;
all that is wrong he setteth right."

Returning to earth, the Glendoveer found
Ladurlad and Kailyal where the great Rajah
had left them.

Stretching out her hand to warn him against
nearer approach, the maiden said : "Strange
things have befallen us, dear Ereenia, since
you left us.   The Almighty Man has sued for
peace.   It is written on my forehead, he says,
that he and I, alone of all mortals, must drink
the Amreeta cup of immortality.   And so he
would have had me share his throne in the

paradise of Swerga. I need not tell you my answer. You see here in this leprosy his revenge."

The Glendoveer answered : " Be sure, dear maiden—dearer now than ever—be sure that he has not read the book of fate aright. Did he say the Amreeta cup? So far, doubtless, he has been able to discover the secret of the future ; for fate reveals some things, and some she hides. To Yamen we must go; this is Seeva's own decree. It is he, the righteous power of death, who will redress our wrongs; and it is Yamen who keeps the Amreeta cup."

So the Glendoveer and Ladurlad and Kailyal went, obedient to Seeva's command, along the dreary road which leads to the dwelling of Yamen. Many days they journeyed, till they came to where the outer ocean encompasses the earth. Not like other seas was this ocean, rather like an abyss on whose brink they stood ; for it was hidden in a darkness which the sun could not pierce, and in which neither moon nor stars were to be seen.

In a creek of this strange sea there lay at anchor a ship as strange, to convey these pilgrims across the deep. Its sides were leaky, and let in the waves ; its mast was broken, and its one sail tattered. But it was useless to delay upon the shore. And, indeed, there sounded through the darkness an awful voice, bidding them embark. So, with a prayer for protection, they took their seats. Self-hoisted, the sail spread itself to the wind ; hands that they could not see loosed the cable, and so they started on their voyage, leaving the day behind them.

The ship sped swift as an arrow across the sea ; and as it sped Ladurlad felt the curse leave his heart and his brain, and Kailyal was free again of the hideous defilement of the leprosy. "The Almighty Man has no dominion here," she cried.

Reaching the other shore, they found the gulf which was the road to the dwelling of Yamen. Round its brink stood the souls of the dead ; and ever and anon the Genii who are the ministers of the god rose out of the darkness, and catching those souls whose hour was come that they should be judged, plunged with them into the deep.

"Those Genii," said the Glendoveer to Ladurlad, "wonder to see us here ; but they come
for the dead and not for us. Fear them not.
A little while you must be left alone, while I
bear your daughter down to Yamen's seat."

So speaking he took Kailyal in his arms,
and saying, "Beloved, be of good courage ;
it is I !" plunged into the darkness of the
gulf.

Padalon, the abode of death, had eight gates,
and at each gate a heavenly guard, always at
his post. At one of these gates the Glendoveer
laid his charge, who, pale and cold with fear,
hung an almost lifeless weight about his neck.

"Who art thou," said the guardian, " son of
light, that comest at this portentous hour, when
Yamen's throne is trembling, and we can scarcely
hinder the rebel race from seizing Padalon ?
Who art thou, and why bringest thou hither
this mortal maid, fitter for the Swerga than for
this doleful scene ? "

"Lord of the gate," said the Glendoveer,
"we come in obedience to Seeva's high command. He, to whom the secrets of the future
are known, bade us come hither. We should

find justice, he said, by Yamen's throne. And
now I leave this maiden under thy charge;
keep her, while I mount to bring her father
down."

Then turning to Kailyal: " Be brave; I
shall be here anon," and spreading his wings
for flight, sprang up.

For a moment the maiden stood gazing after
him, with straining eyes and outstretched arms.
She would fain have called him back; but,
gathering up all her courage, she checked the
cry, and crossing her patient arms, sat at the
feet of the guardian of the gate, prepared to
meet what the will of the gods might bring.

The guardian's brow relaxed as he looked
upon her; and hope, long unfelt in his heart,
revived. " Now may the blessing of the
Powers of Padalon be on thee!" he cried; " and
blessed be the hour which gave thee birth!
Thou hast brought hope, too long a stranger,
to these drear abodes; for surely Nature cannot have made thee to be aught but an in-
heritor of heaven."

And he looked at the maiden with a smile,
thinking that Seeva had sent her to be the

messenger of hope and deliverance from Kehama's unrighteous power.

Meanwhile the Glendoveer had returned, bringing Ladurlad with him. And the three stand before the gate.

"Guardian of the gate," said the Glendoveer, "I come, as I have said, by Seeva's own command; tell me the way to Yamen's throne."

"Bring forth the chariot," said the guardian.

And the chariot was brought, self-moving, poised upon a single wheel. And next two mantles were brought, white and shining as snow. In these father and child were arrayed; for so only could their mortal flesh and blood endure the way.

So the three mounted the chariot, and it rolled through the gate of Padalon, and went on its way till it came to Yamen's palace. The guards who kept the palace gave way before it, till it brought them to the very presence of the god.

On a marble sepulchre he sat, and at his feet the righteous Baly had his judgment-seat. Before him three human figures supported a golden throne, with their hands outspread, and their shoulders bowed beneath the weight. A vacant place was left, which a fourth bearer was yet to fill.

Alighting from the car, the Glendoveer did homage to the god; then, raising his head, said: "We come as suppliants to thy throne. We need not tell thee the wrongs for which we seek redress. Thou knowest them already. We come by Seeva's own command."

"It is well," said Yamen; "the hour is near when fate will reveal its secrets. Not lightly did the Wisest send his suppliants hither, where we, in doubt and fear, attend the awful issue. Wait ye, also, in faith and patience for the End."

CHAPTER VI.

As Yamen spoke, there fell a sudden silence throughout the doleful region of death, a silence more awful than all the cries of lamentation and despair which had been heard before. Then through the silence there was heard an unwonted sound, that grew deeper as it advanced. It was the sound of Kehama's approach, for now all the rites of sacrifice and penance had been accomplished, and he came in the fulness of his power to seize on the throne of Padalon.

In all his might and majesty he came; and, by the attribute of deity which he had won from heaven, he came self-multiplied, assailing the fortress of Yamen on every side at once. At each of the eight gates he stood at one and the same time, and beat down the eight guardians under his feet, and then in his brazen chariots of triumph drove through each gate at the same moment. Each chariot was drawn by a hundred aulays, creatures bigger than the biggest elephant, ten yokes of ten abreast. So he passed on in his strength to the throne of Yamen himself.

Then Yamen put forth all his strength to do battle with his enemy. A darkness, thicker than the blackest night, concealed their strife ; but, when it cleared away, it was seen that the might of sacrifice had prevailed. The Rajah was triumphant ; and absorbing again his many shapes into one, he took his seat on the marble sepulchre, with the conquered Yamen's neck under his feet.

He sat silent, a smile upon his lips, dallying with his power, as a guest at some rich banquet sips once and again from the goblet before he drains it. Before him stood the golden throne. He could not choose but see it, and seeing it could not but wonder.

"Who are ye," he cried, "that in such torment bear this throne of gold ? And why are ye but three ?   And for whom is the fourth place reserved ? "

The first bearer said : " I was the first of men to heap superfluous wealth, adding store to store which I needed not."

The second said : " I was the first of men to usurp power that was not mine, to set up a throne as king and conqueror."

The third said : " I was the first of men that imposed upon mankind a tale of falsehood in the name of God.   Here we have stood for ages tormented, and still we are but three. A fourth will come to share our torment, to bear at yonder vacant corner his portion of the burden.   Thus it has been appointed ; and he must be equal in guilt to us.   Come, Kehama, we have waited for thee too long."

And all three took up the words like a choral song : " Kehama, Almighty Man, we have waited for thee too long !"

A laugh of wondering pride burst from him. He deigned to make no reply ; but, with an altered look, he turned to Kailyal.   " Maiden," he said, " thou seest how idle it is to seek escape from the devices of fate.   Thou hast fled to Yamen's throne, and lo! I am here. We two are destined to share the Amreeta cup of immortality. Then join thy hand in mine with a willing heart."

" It cannot be," said she. " Almighty as thou art, still the heart and will are free."

" Once more bethink thee," said the Rajah. " Take thy seat upon this throne, Kehama's willing bride, and I will place all the kingdoms of the world beneath thy father's feet. Refuse, and he shall stand for ever its fourth supporter."

" I have spoken," said Kailyal; and Ladurlad caught her proudly in his arms.

" Bring forth the Amreeta cup," said Kehama to Yamen.

" It is within the sepulchre," replied the god; " bid it be opened."

" Give up thy treasure," cried the Almighty Man to the marble sepulchre; and at his word it opened wide, and showed a huge skeleton within holding the cup in its hand.

" Give me the cup," Kehama cried again; and, obedient to his word, the ghastly shape arose, and gave the Amreeta into the Rajah's hands.

"Drink," it said; "for thee only and for Kailyal, of all the children of mankind, is the cup designed by Fate."

"This is the end," cried, with heart elate, the Almighty Man. "Now have I triumphed over death. Henceforth I wage war with thee, Seeva, on equal terms, a god against a god."

And he raised to his lips the fatal bowl.

Thus far the Glendoveer had stood, still strong in faith, even when he saw the Lord of Padalon beaten down under the Rajah's feet. He had hoped to see Seeva put forth his destroying might. But now, when he saw Kehama stand with the cup in his hand, he resolved to dare the conflict. But, as he sprang forward, the skeleton barred his way, and from the throne of gold the three renewed their strain: "Kehama, come ; we wait for thee too long."

In the madness of his wickedness, not knowing the mystery of the cup, that its quality is as the lips that drink it, a blessing to the good, a curse to the evil, Kehama drank.

Then Seeva opened on the accursed man his eye of wrath. He shuddered, but it was too late ; the deed was done. He is immortal now, and immortal he must remain. The Amreeta runs like a stream of poison through his veins.

Then the three take up again their strain: "Come, brother; we have waited for thee too long; too long we have borne the unequal burden. Come, brother, we are four."

Vain was his almighty power. A mightier pain subdued it. He yielded to the bony hand the cup, still unemptied, and took his stand at the vacant corner. Then on the golden throne, at last complete, Yamen took his seat.

The skeleton exclaimed: " For two only of mankind has the Amreeta cup been reserved. The man has drunk; now comes the woman's turn. Come, Kailyal, come, and receive the doom of Heaven."

Wonder and fear and awe perplexed her when she heard; but hope still rose triumphant over all. With trembling hands she took the fated cup, and drank.

And Seeva turned upon her the eye of mercy, and all that was earthly melted from her, and left the pure heavenly soul.

"Go," said Yamen, " Daughter of Earth, that art become the child of Heaven; go, and with thy heavenly lover, in the bowers of Swerga, enjoy a happiness that shall know no end."

But Kailyal still lingered, and keeping her human love and pity, stretched out her hands to her father.

"Go," said Yamen again; "thou shalt find him above in thy mother's bower."

Thus saying, he reached out his hand and laid it gently on Ladurlad's head. He sank to sleep as peacefully as sinks a child, and woke again amidst those whom he loved in the Swerga bowers.

UNWIN BROTHERS, THE GRESHAM PRESS, CHILWORTH AND LONDON.